Oradell at Sea

Also By Meredith Sue Willis:

A Space Apart
Higher Ground
Only Great Changes
Personal Fiction Writing
Blazing Pencils
Quilt Pieces (With Jane Wilson Joyce)
Deep Revision
The Secret Super Powers of Marco
Marco's Monster
In the Mountains of America
Trespassers

Vandalia Press publishes fiction and non-fiction of interest to the general reader concerning Appalachia and, more specifically, West Virginia. See our website at vandaliapress.com to learn of forthcoming titles.

Oradell at Sea

A Novel By

Meredith Sue Willis

Vandalia Press

Morgantown 2002

Vandalia Press, Morgantown 26506
© 2002 by West Virginia University Press
All rights reserved
First edition 2002
Printed in the United States of America
10 09 08 07 06 05 04 03 02   10 9 8 7 6 5 4 3 2 1

ISBN 0-937058-69-6

LIBRARY OF CONGRESS CATALOGING-IN-PUBLICATION DATA

Meredith Sue Willis 1946 -
   Oradell at Sea/Meredith Sue Willis
   000 p. 00 cm.

Library of Congress Control Number: 2002108436

Vandalia Press is an imprint of West Virginia University Press

Book design by Alcorn Publication Design
Illustrations by Ken Kreider
Cover photo of train, courtesy of West Virginia and Regional History Collection,
      WVU Libraries
Printed in USA

Acknowledgments

A portion of Chapter Two appeared as "A Dream of West Fork" in *The Iron
Mountain Review: Meredith Sue Willis Issue,* volume 12, Spring 1996.
(Department of English, Box 64, Emory & Henry College, Emory, VA 24327.)

A different version of Chapter Seven was published as a short story called
"Like a Darkness on Her Heart" in *Vandalia: The Literary Publication of West
Virginia Wesleyan College,* Vol. 1, Spring 2001. (West Virginia Wesleyan
College, Buckhannon, WV 26201.)

To my menfolk, Andy and Joel

- 1 -

*O*radell Greengold would have been a better woman if she had drunk less and been more patient in her life. She might have been a better dressed woman if she hadn't loved red and purple and big earrings, but, all in all, although she did not consider herself particularly good, she did consider herself lucky.

Her father froze to death in an alley, drunk, but he had done his best for her as long as he could. She had a good woman friend back home in West Fork, West Virginia, who taught her how to use sanitary napkins at the right time, and she had been born early enough to cheer our boys in World War Two, but late enough to get a kick out of Elvis Presley. She had had the privilege of being married to Mike Brown, and she had a sweetheart of a son named Lance. Finally, Morris Greengold had been so old when he met Oradell that he never noticed she was no spring chicken either. It was Morris who made her rich, and now she was traveling on Morris's money on the cruise ship *Golden Argonaut* from Acapulco through the Panama Canal to San Juan, Puerto Rico.

Her hair grayed early, her legs and arms stayed thin, and her midsection got big. She stopped smoking once to save money and never started again. Smoking ruined her skin, but not her teeth. She lost a tooth because of the only man who ever hit her, Harry the Ape, but she ran out on him, and he gave her Lance.

Her biggest good luck, Morris Greengold, had come late, when she was working at the Athens Brothers Diner on upper Madison Avenue in New York City. Morris used to come in once a month or so, then once a week, and finally he started having dinner there every night. The Athens Brothers ran a good restaurant, which was one of the reasons she always chose Greek-run cruise ships.

Back then, when she met Morris, she had been feeling grim about the future. She had thought she was through with attracting sober men, so she had been slow on the uptake, that Morris was always at her table, that his jokes got personal. But it sank in after a while, and she went out with him, and he gave her gifts, and his kids hated her, so he decided they should get married. She did things Morris's way till he died, and he left her with more money than she had ever dreamed of. She lived in resorts and on cruise ships, keeping an apartment in New York for herself and Lance. She especially loved the *Golden Argonaut* where they made your bed and fed you. They came when you called, at any hour.

She always told her assigned dinner partners that the *Golden Argonaut* was the perfect cruise ship, plenty elegant, but not too big. She spoke from experience because she had sailed on the best. The exact way she liked to introduce herself was to be the first seated—coming in early on the arm of one of the waiters. It used to be

Stavros who brought her in, but Stavros had worked his way up to Assistant Chief of Housekeeping and part-time bartender. So tonight he walked her to the door of the dining room where he handed her over to Nikko, the youngest and tallest of the waiters. Stavros carefully removed her hand from his arm and put it on Nikko's.

Nikko smiled down at her Hong Kong silk sheath dress in a red bougainvillea blossom print and said, "You look so beautiful, Mrs. Oradell."

And she said, "Nice to be back, boys. Nikko, honey, I think you grew since last summer."

"I grew fatter, Mrs. Oradell," he said. "You want another drink?"

She gave his ribs a pat and said yes, but was distracted by a trim gray-haired couple who had already arrived at her table. So she wasn't going to be first. She liked to be first, but at least it was her favorite table, on the starboard side near the windows giving on the deep blue of the ocean and a vast low Pacific sunset. The couple rose in their seats respectfully, and she liked that. Oradell greeted them like she was Tallulah Bankhead. She could keep this up for a while, if she had had just the right number of drinks. She had perfected several little speeches, and she could drawl them out without a hint of hillbilly or Yiddish or street Spanish. She could manage this for periods of up to two minutes, if she could have the floor to herself. People usually gave it to her, at least on the first night of a cruise.

One of the stories she told sometimes, when she got to know people better, was how Harry the Ape, Lance's father, used to fix his hands around her neck and squeeze gently, like it was a joke but not really: I'll do it Oradell, he whispered, I will. Someday I'll do it. And the point of her story was that after incident number two, which was accompanied by the sock to the jaw that loosened a tooth, she had stopped wearing necklaces and started saving half her tips and stealing from his wallet, and eventually bought the fourth-hand Ford that nobody else in the entire city of Las Vegas wanted, and she took Lance and left.

You got to fish or cut bait, Oradell liked to say. I ain't always fished so good, but I know'd how to cut bait. By this time, if she told this story, she knew the people well enough to use any accent or phrase she had picked up in her entire life from Appalachia to Nevada to the French Riviera and New York City.

The gray-haired couple were angular with big white smiles. They sat down when she sat down. The man was wearing more jewelry than the woman, and their name was Blume. They said they were from Houston, but they didn't sound Texan. That's America for you, thought Oradell, Chicago Texans and New York hillbillies. She looked around for Nikko and her drink. There would be six altogether at her table, just the right number. Eight was too many. When she decided to be outrageous, she liked to see the effect on each person.

Nikko brought her a goblet of iced gin with a shave of lemon. A Tanqueray gin martini on the rocks with lemon and hold the vermouth.

The Blumes were apologetic about getting into the dining room early—they had come through a side door by mistake, they said, but the waiters were so friendly, they let them go ahead and sit down.

Oradell said, "Oh, all the stewards and waiters on the *Golden Argonaut* are good boys. That was Nikko who brought me my drink. He's the baby. He isn't our waiter, though. We have Jaime. A little surly, but real efficient."

She had a couple of stories about Jaime to tell too, if she got in the mood. Jaime owed her for not getting him in trouble last summer. Not that the knife had been very big, but he had waved it in Oradell's direction. Jaime, in spite of having a wife and five kids in Arecibo, Puerto Rico, always fell in love with the newest boy on the ship. Nikko had been very clear about not going that way, but Jaime was jealous anyhow, so there had been the incident in the corridor when he thought Oradell had Nikko in her room. Never a dull moment, she thought, smiling at the Blumes, holding her stories in reserve.

She guessed the Blumes to be here for good, clean fun. They wore their clothes well, and they had let their hair stay natural: no stupid implants or odd combings to hide what was bald. When they asked where she was from, she gave one of her prepared speeches: "I'm from the high seas, darlin'. I live to cruise. I keep a hotel room in L.A. and a *peed-a-teer* in New York, as the French say, but my real home is right here."

"On the *Golden Argonaut*?" said Ilene Blume.

Which was exactly what Oradell had meant, but she said, "Wherever I happen to be, honey."

The doors opened, and the crowd buzzed in. "Here they come!" said Oradell. "Now those two gentlemen over there, coming in together? That's the Retired Naval Officers, Johnny and Clyde. Johnny is just a Host, part of the cruise staff. He's supposed to escort the divorcees and widows. Clyde does a little escorting too, but he's also the ship's doc. That old lady with the pink hair always makes them sit with her. She's a regular on this ship, too, but I've got seniority. Clyde holds his liquor pretty well, but I never thought we'd see Johnny back after last time."

Johnny and Clyde saw her looking at them from across the room and waved, and she waved back. Pinky couldn't see well enough to know someone was waving. Oradell's real favorites weren't the old drunks, though, but the fresh faces, the newest, most recently filthy rich. She was one too, of course, but flattered herself that she had no pretenses. She wasn't ashamed of who she had been. It was prime entertainment to watch the ones she called the Nouveaux. Leading the pack tonight were three couples with blond poodle curls and neck chains over chest hair. They squealed and guffawed. They were here to do it all! Buy emeralds in Cartagena, partner swapping on board. She could already tell she was going to enjoy them. More than the Blumes, who were too decent to be entertaining.

The Nouveaux's table was one over, and she could see the jeweled false nails on the women. Two of them had a single decorative nail with stones, but the loudest and fattest one—also with the biggest hair and deepest décolletage—had ten gold nails.

"Goddam," said Oradell. "Look at that, Blume! That is some conspicuous consumption." She never liked things done halfway. Something settled pleasurably in her. If you were going to drink yourself to death, do it right, like her daddy. If you were going to have false nails, make it ten gold ones.

Mr. Blume said to Oradell, "That's a lovely bracelet you're wearing, Mrs. Greengold," and tapped the one on her left wrist with its thin, overlapped lozenges of gold.

"Oh, Bob," said Ilene, "you shouldn't comment on people's jewelry!"

"I don't mind," said Oradell. "Hell, what's a vacation if you have to watch what you say? I've got lot of jewelry, but my favorite is this little ring." She had to wear it on her little finger now, because her knuckles had got big with age: it was thin and silver with a little red stone.

Blume held her hand and looked at the ring. "Good workmanship."

"I guess it was," she said, "It's lasted through dishwashing and diapers and fistfights and more things than you want to hear about. So I guess it did have good workmanship."

Bob Blume said, "I'm an ophthalmologist, but my father was a jeweler. I spent a lot of time around the business. I have always loved good jewelry, Mrs. Greengold."

"Call me Oradell, honey. Now there's a coincidence, my late husband Morris was a jeweler. Greengold was the right name for him, let me tell you. The stuff he sold turned green in two places: on your neck and in his pocket. He did something in the jewelry district in New York, I never got the details, I assume it was legal because they let me inherit."

"You don't sound like a New Yorker," said Ilene.

She means I don't sound Jewish, thought Oradell. "I lived there near thirty years, honey, but I was born in West Virginia. That's right, West by Gosh Virginia. Home of the Bituminous Coal Miner. They booted me out when I was young and stupid, and I lived all over the country, but I was born in West Fork, West Virginia."

"Coal Miner's Daughter," said Bob Blume.

"I had a granddaddy in the mines, but my own daddy mostly swept out stores. And the story of how I ended up in New York marrying Morris Greengold is too long for first acquaintance, but if things get slow, I'll tell you."

"I'd love to hear it!" said Ilene, too enthusiastically for Oradell's taste.

Making judgements was part of Oradell's fun. Maybe she'd be wrong about the Blumes being boring. Maybe Mrs. B. was an ax murderer and Mr. B. an international jewel thief. Oradell felt good: she liked the sound of voices as people got settled and met each other. She liked the tinkle of glasses and cutlery and the ten gold nails on Miz Chubby Nouveau.

I ought to sleep instead of drinking in the afternoon more often, thought Oradell. Maybe I'll turn over a new leaf.

Jaime came scuttling over to take their bar order. He was short and pudgy with five o'clock shadow, heavy brows, and deep-set eyes. "Hey, Jaime," she said, "How's it hanging? Don't take any wooden knives." He flared his nostrils at her. One thing about Jaime, he didn't bother to butter you up. She'd heard him complaining about something in the corridor earlier today, Spanish too fast to follow.

Bob said he might have another Scotch, it was vacation after all, and then the rest of the table finally arrived, almost the last to come in. It was a threesome, parents and a stunningly lovely adolescent daughter with her arms crossed over her chest in sullen splendor. All three were dressed in fluorescent white. Named Bill and Cathy Weston, the adults about the same age as the Blumes, but with all their hair preserved in blonde. Orange County California Republicans, guessed Oradell.

They put the pouting girl, Tracy, next to Oradell.

Oradell decided that if they were even the least bit stuffy, she would tell them straight out that her son Lance was a female impersonator. This wasn't strictly speaking true. He would have liked to be that, probably, but he had gotten out of performing a while ago and was mostly trying, at least in theory, to be a producer.

The waiters were still seating the latecomers and filling bar orders. The Westons chatted up the Blumes. The teeny-bopper sneered at her plate and clutched her own arms. Oradell was just beginning to get bored when the captain came through the door.

"Here comes the Old Man," she said. "He doesn't hang out a lot with the guests because he don't speaka da English so much, but he's a good man. The weasel beside him is named Reese. He's supposed to be working for the new company that bought the *Golden Argonaut*. He's making sure nobody steals the spoons."

The Blumes smiled at Oradell with their enthusiastic big teeth, and the Westons looked around the room, as if hoping to see an old friend. The company man, Reese, wore a small tan moustache and uniform whites, but no insignia, and sounded like an American. Oradell had had a run-in with him earlier in the day. She had caught him dressing down Stavros for getting her extra pillows. She had set Reese straight all right. The Captain led the way now, coming from table to table, crisp in white with gold epaulets, moving gracefully, like a ship himself: face broad and purple, jowls trembling. "Apoplectic," said Oradell. "Poor Old Man is looking very apoplectic."

The Captain bowed, then kissed Oradell's hand and said mournfully, "Aha Missus. So beautiful like always. Happy, happy, happy."

She introduced the others to him. "Mr. and Mrs. Blume, and the Weston Family," she said.

"So happy to meet," said the Captain. "So happy happy."

"*Kali nikta*," said Oradell showing off her Athens Brothers Diner Greek, which always made the Captain sigh and kiss her hand again. The cruise staff, the entertainment people who arranged the on-shore tours and ran the boutiques, were Americans, but the actual crew, from the Old Man on down, were Greek, Lebanese, or Maltese, with a handful of Puerto Ricans.

"How many languages do you speak, Oradell?" asked Ilene.

"Just English, honey, but I can cuss in seven."

The shrimp cocktails arrived. Oradell said, "The Captain never hurries. If it gets rough, he doesn't mind falling a little behind schedule. He'll aim into the waves for a few hours so the ship won't roll so bad. A couple of cruises ago, we had a real rough trip, a lot of old people broke things."

The Blumes looked up, smiling, expecting amusing stories. Mr. Weston said, "These shrimps aren't all that big."

But Mrs. Weston—Cathy—had decided to be polite to Oradell. "Broke things?" she said.

"Arms, legs, a dislocated shoulder."

"That's terrible!" said Ilene Blume.

"Us old folks is frail, honey."

"You're not old, Oradell!" Bob Blume might be boring, but he was a gentleman.

"So the captain, just to show you, he didn't cart off the old folks, he got a team of orthopedists flown in from Caracas, and they splinted 'em up, relocated the shoulders, and they all finished the trip. I don't think the company liked it, though, because that cost a pretty penny. The Old Man don't care, he wants his folks to enjoy their cruise. That's the kind of fellow he is."

"How awful," said Cathy.

Oradell grinned. There's more where that came from. honey, she thought. I've got some stories that'll take that yaller dye right out of your hair.

The Westons and the Blumes started talking about where they lived. Oradell hated talks about houses and communities. And it turned out that the Westons, from La Jolla, not only liked to talk about houses, they developed subdivisions. And their own subdivision—Sea Breezes or Best View or Top o' the Heap or something like that—was the *crème de la crème* of choice areas. "The trick with selling houses in the La Jolla area," said Cathy, "isn't finding buyers. It's finding people who want to sell. Everyone wants to live in La Jolla."

Oradell watched the teenager, Tracy, practice curling her lip and nibbling a roll at the same time. Look at that skin, she thought. Angel skin. She wondered idly if this was the moment to bring up Lance's profession.

Cathy Weston had moved on to how much she loved tennis. She was looking desperately for partners whenever they got to someplace with courts. And lo and behold, both of the Blumes played. But Bill Weston had a bad knee and had to forgo it. In fact, that was why they were taking a cruise this winter instead of something more active.

Oradell said, "You won't be getting in much tennis till we get through the Panama Canal. But just the same you're going to like the *Golden Argonaut*. Nice and small. Just the right size. Some of the big ones are too big.

Cunard, Royal, Royal Viking. Not that they aren't good lines. They're very good lines, but they're big. I went around-the-world the first year I started." One by one they turned to her as she kept her volume up.

Only Bill Weston ignored her. "The shrimps are small, but they don't have that iodine taste."

"The big ships," said Oradell, "have everything planned for you." She waited for the others to break in with a contradiction, and then realized with triumph that neither the Blumes nor the Westons had cruised before. "Too organized," she said. "It's like some kind of summer camp. Some of them have their own medical specialists onboard, if there are a lot of old folks cruising. And the biggest ones have special freezers for the bodies."

Cathy Weston's eyes popped, but it was the little girl who really perked up. "Dead bodies?"

"Yep, that long a cruise, you have to plan ahead. We lost five that trip."

Blume gave a little whistle.

The girl said, "You mean they, like, freeze the bodies?"

"Well, honey, what would you do? They had to make sure they'd keep till we got to a port and they could fly 'em home."

Ilene Blume gave a half-suppressed giggle. "I suppose they could be buried at sea."

Bob said, "It wouldn't be the worst way to go."

"I'm going to die at sea," said Oradell.

Cathy Weston gave her a look that intimated anytime tomorrow before dinner would be just fine.

The Westons latched onto the Blumes now, one-on-one, Bill asking Bob Blume medical questions,

Cathy working her diamond bracelet up and down her arm and telling Ilene Blume her problems.

Oradell leaned across the table and interrupted. "Nice bracelet, Cathy. What do you think of it, Blume? Blume grew up in the jewelry business, and I inherited it. Where did you get yours, Weston?"

"My what?"

"Your moolah, honey. Your bucks."

"We told you," murmured Cathy, "we do real estate."

"Yeah, but if you're a developer, you got it from somewhere. You don't start with nothing." She had a feeling she was getting too far out, a little too much iced gin making the air gelid between her and them. If she wasn't careful, they would write her off as a drunk and ignore her for the rest of the trip. "Don't answer that," she said. "Old Oradell's just jawboning."

She made an effort then to shut up through the main course while Weston went on about how much you can jack up the price of houses if the development has tennis courts. And Cathy Weston explaining in more detail about Bill's knee and how they wouldn't have come on the *Golden Argonaut* at all, otherwise.

Oradell ate her chicken and drank another Tanqueray and speculated about the Westons' little vacation. She decided it wasn't Bill's knee but the girl. She was more or less the age Oradell had been when she married Mike Brown. A sexy age, all the hormones kicking in. The girl ate too much to be anorexic. No, thought Oradell, it had been the wrong boyfriend. Or drugs. Or an abortion. Maybe all three. That was why the Westons were taking the cruise in the middle of the school year.

She was tired by the time Jaime came to tell about dessert. "Send the biggest slice of chocolate cake you have to my room, sweetie," she told him, "and a pot of black coffee. I'm going to go drink and eat cake." She stood up and addressed her table. "It's great being rich, honey," she said. "You can do any damn thing you please."

- 2 -

*O*radell was in bed waiting for Stavros. She had a glass ashtray full of aspirins for her headaches. She had her own refrigerator with juice, ice, seltzer, and bottles of cold gin—not minis stolen from airlines either: three beautiful rounded green bottles of Tanqueray, plus Chopin Polish vodka. If she didn't use up the liquor by the end of the cruise, she gave it to the staff. She liked to give things away, and she liked to tip.

When he arrived, fully dressed in a clean white jacket, she said, "Sorry to call you at this hour, Stavros. "I can't sleep. I guess I haven't settled in yet."

He had smooth short hair: a small, neat man who had looked the same as long as she'd known him, smooth faced like a kid, but in his late thirties at least, and probably forty. "What do you want to drink?" he asked her. "Something healthy?" He started mixing ice and seltzer, orange juice and vodka. "It takes a day or two to settle."

She said, "I don't know anything about you, Stavros. All these years, and you're still a mystery to me. I know all about grouchy old Jaime and his wife and five *niños*.

But you, I don't even know if you have a family back in Greece."

"Everybody has a family, Mrs. Oradell."

"But you don't tell anybody what you do when you aren't on the *Golden Argonaut*."

"I'm always on the *Golden Argonaut*."

"Well, I know why you were so slow getting here tonight. You were taking care of Pinky."

He smiled just a little. "I take care of everybody, Mrs. Oradell. That's my job. But you're the best."

"Yeah, I bet you tell that to Pinky too. Only the difference between her and me is, she can't hear a thing you or anyone else says. She's going to end up in the cooler one of these trips. Were you changing her hearing aid battery, Stavros? Or just charging her up."

"Everybody is charged up, this trip, Mrs. Oradell. Lots of charges this trip, and too many changes."

"What kind of changes?"

"The company decided to down-staff. They looking for people to fire. You remember that nice boy I brought you from the engine room last summer?"

"The little small one with the crooked smile? They fired him?"

Stavros shrugged and handed her the drink. "Laid off. They cut out everywhere except the waiters and stewards, and we got extra work. They don't want the guests to notice. Everybody hurry, hurry. Work faster."

"Sounds like a factory instead of a cruise ship."

While she sipped her drink, Stavros leaned against the wall of the closet. His eyelids drooped. He snapped them open and yawned. "You want a boy, Mrs. Oradell?"

"I don't think so," she said. "I think I'll give up men. To tell you the truth, I always liked men, but sometimes you get tired of a good thing. Don't take it personal."

"You know me, Mrs. Oradell, I get you what you want. Engine room boys, waiters—"

"Why don't you sit down, Stavros?" He shrugged and sat on the other bed. She was talking to keep him awake. For company. She said, "Maybe I was always a lesbian and never knew it. I mean, there's something kinky about me, isn't there?"

"You are one fine woman, Mrs. Oradell."

She liked the lively taste of the carbonated orange juice with just a touch of vodka to ease the likelihood of headache. She liked to talk in the night with low lights. Sometimes Stavros curled up on the second bed and fell asleep if she talked long enough. But he didn't lie down tonight. "I don't know, Stavros, I'm tired. I don't have so much energy."

"You have plenty of pep, Mrs. Oradell."

"I need to relax this trip."

"So," Stavros yawned. "I have relaxing boys. You want to relax with one of the boys tonight?"

"Not tonight. I want some more pillows. In spite of that goddam Reese. I couldn't believe him, telling you not to get me my pillows. Would you mind a lot, going out and getting me two more?" He shrugged again, went out, came back with more pillows. "If Reese finds out," she said, "send him to me."

Stavros tucked them behind her. She stuck her foot out from under the covers, and he sat down on the edge of the bed, started to massage her instep. He said, "How about Georgi from housekeeping? You used to like him."

"His breath got bad. Leave me alone about the boys, Stavros. Another night, maybe. I don't like the those California people at my table. I don't mind a good old fashioned Calvin Coolidge Republican, but I can't stand these greasy greedy ones who think they deserve everything they got. They look at me like I was a bad smell."

She sighed with the pressure on her foot. Stavros was relaxing just to look at too, everything about him was neat. He had short legs, and his round head was balding, but what hair was left was good and dense. He had never been her type, but he had a kind touch.

He said, "Your American political parties, Mrs. Oradell, all the same."

"Not true. The Democrats are corrupt as hell but they have warm hearts. You know what I mean? John L. Lewis of the United Mineworkers went with the Democrats, except when he was mad at FDR. Big John was as corrupt as the next one, but it's one thing to belly up to the trough like the Democrats do and make room for everybody. The Democrats like a crowd. And the old-fashioned Republicans, they used to be at least nice clean people who practiced what they preached. It's these new ones I can't stand. They enjoy their slop more if there's somebody hungry watching them eat."

"Mrs. Oradell, you want a bath tonight?"

"I don't know," she said. "I'm already in my night gown."

"I get you fresh," said Stavros. "You got so many."

She said, "Did I ever say you look like Peter Lorre?"

He tucked her feet back under the covers and opened her night gown drawer and held up a pink nightie over his chest. "You like this?"

"No, I want the green one with the unbleached lace. I bet you don't even know who Peter Lorre is."

"Old time movie star," said Stavros. "This one?"

"That's the one." She could never understand how a man like Stavros had learned what he learned. She herself had dropped out of high school and never had time for books, but she always read magazines: women's magazines, men's magazines, movie magazines, *Life* and *National Geographic* magazines, *Time* and *Newsweek*. Anything with pictures and not too thick.

She said, "How come you put me at Jaime's table and not Nikko's?"

"Jaime is a good waiter."

"Oh, Jaime can pass out the grub. Nothing against Jaime, except that he always looks like he's planning to slit your throat. Especially if he's in love. I hope he's not in love."

"Not this trip. No new hires." He filled a plastic basin of water in the bathroom, brought it out and her washcloth and a stack of thick white towels. He hummed to himself. Oradell felt the motion of the ship, the distant hum of the engines. She had her extra pillows and now her extra extra pillows. Stavros would give her a sponge bath, change her nightie, put her in the fresh bed.

He washed her feet first, worked up each leg, lots of towels, big, thick towels on the *Golden Argonaut*. He wiped her arms, her fingers.

She looked at her arm, loose skin around the elbow. "I don't know, Stavros," she said. "I'm not what I once was. When I first came on the *Golden Argonaut*, you couldn't get enough boys for me. I was a regular nympho."

"You're still a regular nympho, Mrs. Oradell." He laid out two towels and lifted her in his arms onto them, like a baby, to wash her middle.

"I took care of myself when I was three years old," she said. "Three years old and I was already taking care of myself and my father both. You think I'm exaggerating. You think I'm just a rich bitch like those Nouveaux Republicans, but I'm playing catch-up, trying to get my share before I die. I don't do nothing for nobody but me these days. I mean it. Just me."

Very careful, spilling almost none, he sponged and trickled warm water over her middle. "Mrs. Oradell," he said, "you tipping every day this time or the end of the cruise? Some of the boys ask me to ask you."

"Not you?" she said. "You wouldn't ask for yourself, would you? You're all money grubbers. You don't love me, just my money."

"Ah, Mrs. Oradell. You're the best. Money is only the ice cream on the cake."

"Yeah? Well, what if I had no money like I did ninety per cent of my life? What if I lost it tomorrow? Would you come in here and give me 3 a.m. sponge baths?"

Very sincerely, he said, "We'd take good care of you. We like you, Mrs. Oradell."

"Maybe, but you wouldn't come in at any 3 a.m. for free. Not that I would either. But about the tips, I don't care. When do you want it?"

"Me, I like the end of the cruise. It's like holiday gift, you know? Georgi, if he comes up, you better give him a little each time, keep him coming back."

"What are you doing with all your money, Stavros?"

Stavros said, "I'm saving up. I'm getting me a restaurant someday."

"Where?" she asked. He went back for fresh, warmer water. He bundled her in towels now, so cozy. Stavros would get her vibrations in tune with the ship's engines, with the waves, and she would sleep. Some of the voyages, she had slept straight through every night by the second week. She said, "Where are you going to have your restaurant? Are you going to jump ship and go to New York?"

He emptied the basin and didn't answer.

"If you go to New York, I know some people. Those Greek boys I used to work for, they'll tell you what you need to know. Very nice boys. They know the ropes, like they get their paper goods at some special place in Astoria, Queens. If you start a restaurant in New York, you need to know things like that."

"You gonna stake me, Mrs. Oradell?" he said, bringing the nightgown. He sat down on the edge of her bed again and started rubbing her with the towels. "You gonna make investment in me?"

"No, Stavros, like I said, I only take care of myself. Just me. I'm going to spend every penny Morris left me. Besides, you ought to start your restaurant back home in Athens—"

"Chios," he said, beginning to rinse her belly again. "That's my place. Much smaller. It don't smell like diesel all the time. The most beautiful island."

"Go back home, Stavros. While you're still young. You need too much money to get rich. You know what I mean?"

"Some guys, start with nothing and have big luck."

"Not many. If you win the lottery—"

"I play every time."

"Or you get someone to stake you. Like you said. I mean it, Stavros, I'd be carrying trays on 96th Street and Madison Avenue if it wasn't for luck. One day I would have dropped over because I couldn't carry another tray, and they'd take me to Bellevue. Do these California Republicans work harder than me when I was carrying those trays? Do they work harder than you, Stavros?"

"I don't mind hard work, Mrs. Oradell. You invest in my restaurant, you see how I work."

"You take my advice, and if you don't get lucky soon, go home." She wasn't sure what her point was anymore. Everything was fuzzy. She was warm and buffeted. Something in the stem of her brain smoothed out. She had a vague warm mental image of something different than luck and taking care of yourself. Something from far back, men and women together, lots of them. Not sex, but the way Mike Brown talked. She and Mike were going to travel the United States to make luck for everyone.

She could feel the extra warmth where his hands pressed her through the cloth. She said, "Rub me bald, Stavros, baby."

"You already bald down there, Mrs. Oradell."

"Don't get fresh."

Rubbing and rubbing, his sturdy little fingers. He put her into the fresh nightgown. He opened up the fresh bed, he tucked her in, remade the other bed while she drifted off, finally turned off the overhead light.

She had a dream she called the Dead Miner. It was about West Fork, West Virginia, where she grew up. When she thought of West Fork in conscious memory, it was green and damp or winter black with ice floes in the river. But in her dream, the weather was yellow and dry. In her dream a monstrous statue called the Dead Miner had toppled, and it filled the town like a Mount

Rushmore giant. The Dead Miner had something to do with the Great West Fork Mine Explosion, which had happened long before she was born.

The Explosion was the only thing West Fork was famous for, the thing Oradell and the other kids grew up hearing about, the subject of their daydreams and nightmares. When she was very small, she had thought death and the Explosion were the same thing. Her mother died when she was small, so for years she thought her mother died in the Explosion. The old dog she played with died, so that must be the Explosion too. She would go up to the gate near the mine portals and squint through the fence, looking for her mother and her dog. In fact, of her family, only her mother's father died among the hundreds in the Explosion.

In her dream, the Dead Miner lay in the middle of West Fork. His heel was shoved into the mine portal, and one knee stuck up into the sky. His enormous face was downtown near the Company store, turned towards the dreamer. It was yellow-brown, with dust on the cheeks and chunks like sleep matter in the corners of the eyes. Out of his great nostrils and eyes granules of sand trickled and gathered momentum as they flowed. He grew larger as she watched, filling her dream vision, threatening to choke her with his crying sand.

She woke sucking for air and rearranged her pillows. The Dead Miner was her grandfather she never met. Or maybe he was her father, frozen stiff behind the Company Store. Or maybe he was her first husband, Mike Brown.

Maybe he was all of the ones who died with no luck at all.

- 3 -

*O*radell was almost adopted by the Talkington family when she was eleven. The crisis came at the end of the year her dad Hugh Riley stayed dry for nine months and got religion. That year he washed and shaved every day and was a janitor at the Baptist Church as well as at the Company store. Oradell had a good year too. She was in the Christmas performance at school, and Hugh came to see her. She made her best grades ever, especially in arithmetic and elocution, but she did just fine in spelling and Colonial Times too. Neither she nor her dad cussed or smoked or chewed tobacco even when they were having supper alone. Hugh was putting by money to take Oradell on a big shopping spree. He was going to buy false teeth for himself.

At that age, you are still young enough not to look a gift horse in the mouth. Oradell was so happy with the way things were going that she had decided she would go down the aisle at church to accept Jesus Christ as her personal Lord and Savior. But she waited too long, and Hugh turned up one Sunday morning asleep in the basement stairwell of the church, disheveled and stinking.

After that, things went back to normal for a while, with Hugh drinking and neither one of them going to church. Oradell liked being able to cuss again, but she missed dressing up for Sunday School.

One day Hugh lifted his face off the table while Oradell was sashaying around like a movie star and trying to get a glimpse of herself in the shaving mirror. He said, "Well if that ain't the damnedest thing."

Oradell said, "What's the damnedest thing?"

"You got titties. A scrawny little thing like you, and you're going to have big titties like your ma. And your legs ain't bad either. If I was a artist, I'd paint a picture." Then he fell back to sleep.

If he had stayed awake, she would have yelled at him for making comments about what was no business of his, but he didn't, so Oradell got the dishrag and wrapped it around her waist in a sort of high-rise girdle to see if she could make her breasts look even more like a movie star's.

She and her dad only had the one room with the kitchen table and the stove and the couch where he slept and her cot behind a clothes tree where she hung their clothes and gave herself a little privacy. Usually she liked hearing her father's night time grunts and groans, but this night Oradell came swimming up out of sleep and found him screaming and throwing punches at something invisible. She tried to go back to sleep, but he started kicking over the chairs, so when his back was turned, she ran out and knocked next door at the Pierces. She chose the Pierces, even though they were colored and not very friendly, because both of the grown ups were always sober.

She pounded on their door and cried, "Mrs. Pierce! Mrs. Pierce! My daddy's seeing a ghost!"

Mrs. Pierce came to the door wearing a man's sweater over her nightgown. She took off the sweater when she saw how Oradell was shaking and put it on her. Then she went over to Oradell's house and looked in the window, shook her head, and grunted. "He's having the dee-tees, little girl. There's nobody can do a thing about that except Jesus. Does your daddy talk to Jesus?"

"He did for a while," said Oradell. "But he stopped."

Mrs. Pierce shook her head and grunted some more and said, "Well, I expect you'll have to sleep at my house tonight."

Oradell was afraid of Mr. Pierce, but she was more afraid of the dee-tees, so she went inside. Mrs. Pierce put her on their couch, but made her pray for a while first, both of them down on their knees, and then Oradell on the couch and Mrs. Pierce praying some more. She liked it pretty well and fell asleep to the sound of Mrs. Pierce talking to Jesus. When she woke up, Mr. and Mrs. Pierce were arguing in the kitchen, but then he went to work, and Mrs. Pierce gave Oradell some toast with butter and jelly. She said, "Listen here, little girl, if your daddy goes off with the dee-tees again, pick up your pillow and come on over here."

She did it once more, on a night when she knew Mr. Pierce was working his night job. But then her father ran off, and she went over to live with the Talkingtons, so she didn't have to bother Mrs. Pierce anymore.

Looking back, when she thought about it, it occurred to her that there were people like the Pierces and Talkingtons who took care of her. She had maybe been better off than she thought, back when she used to feel sorry for herself. She was always jealous because

Sarah Ellen Talkington had a big house and a mother and father, and jealous of the Pierce kids because their parents sent them on the street car to Fairmont to the school for colored kids who were going to be leaders of their people someday.

But the truth was, people kept an eye on Oradell, and the Talkingtons were seriously thinking about adopting her. Mr. Talkington, the store manager, and his family lived on the West Side. They owned their house, not the company. A store manager's salary was not really enough to own a home, but Mrs. Talkington was a member of one of the oldest families in Marion County, with an uncle who was a judge and one who wrote for the newspaper. Mrs. Talkington had created a select small society for herself even in the mining town of West Fork. She founded a gardening club and was the president of the Fidelis Class at the Baptist church. They had meetings with refreshments and sometimes discussed the welfare of poor people like the ones out on Shacky Hill where Oradell lived.

The Talkington daughter Sarah Ellen had always been nice to Oradell. If they hadn't been friends, Oradell would never have agreed to try living with her family. Sarah Ellen was pretty to look at and easy to boss around. She giggled whenever Oradell decided to cut up and be silly. Oradell never, from earliest childhood, underestimated the value of a good audience.

She would have preferred to live with Grace Howard, who was on her own side of the river, but Grace couldn't top the Talkingtons' offer which included a private bedroom, a bathroom shared only with Sarah Ellen, and a little light child care from time to time. It was, everyone agreed, just what was needed for Oradell

Riley, a spirited girl who could use some rough edges filed down.

They failed on that score, thought Oradell. They forgot that even a diamond in the rough is still the hardest damn thing around.

So one raw Saturday morning at the end of March, Oradell went to stay with the Talkingtons. She stuffed a pillow case with her underwear and her blanket and slammed the door behind her. There was no key, but since she was still hoping her daddy would come back, she wouldn't have wanted to lock him out anyhow. She was supposed to go to the Company Store and get a lift with Mr. Talkington when he closed up at noon, but she misunderstood and walked all the way to the West Side, carrying her pillow case of clothing.

Oradell was just reaching an age when whole pages suddenly turn over in your mind. She had got her period and her breasts, and her father's defection added to her sense of one door creaking toward closure while other ones opened. This was the first time, for example, that she saw West Fork. That is to say, she saw West Fork every day, but this was the first time she saw it as one whole thing.

She had always known that different people lived in different parts of town: the colored people except for the Pierces lived out the road beyond Shacky Hill; the Italians lived on Mud Street; and the Americans had the other streets. People like the Talkingtons and the mine supervisor and the high school principal and the manager of the movie theater lived on the West Side. But this day, she saw it all in order, spread out before her.

Shacky Hill was one and two-room houses. It was

the only section of West Fork where Italians and Americans and Negroes lived together, because the shacks were so bad that nobody cared who lived there. The only shack that was kept up at all belonged to the Pierces, who were famous for refusing to be segregated. The Pierces were from somewhere else, nobody was sure where, because they didn't talk to anyone. They moved to town during a time when the mines were hiring Negroes, which didn't last long. When Mr. Pierce was laid off, he got a job as janitor at the grade school and a night job as extra janitor at the high school. Mrs. Pierce did special spring cleaning and holiday cleaning for a few people, but she would never accept a job as a domestic for one family alone, and she never took cast off clothes from anybody.

Living in the shacks was regarded as an eccentricity on the part of the Pierce family. Everyone figured the Pierces had to be crazy to live next to white people like Hugh Riley and the Polks. There was an old widow up there too who was just plain destitute, but she hardly ever came out of her house because she was afraid of the Polks. The Polks, stringy haired and red knuckled, quarreled and fought and broke things. They gave Shacky Hill its alternative name, Polkville. They were so outstanding that, in later years, people started using Polkville not just for Shacky Hill but for the whole section of West Fork beyond Mud Street.

That day, nobody was awake at the Polks except three little kids who threw rocks at Oradell and her pillowcase full of clothing. She threw back the same rocks. She saw for the first time how rutted the road was up here, and she saw Mr. Pierce, as usual on a Saturday, out repairing his roof. He frowned at Oradell, and

Oradell frowned back. At the curve in the road, she looked out at the hills surrounding and at the brown swollen West Fork river and the freight trains and the tipple at the mine. She went around the curve and started down Mud Street. In the summer the small houses had vines and flowers, but at this time of year you saw they weren't all that much better than the shacks.

Hugh always promised to show her which house was the one where her mother was born, but he never did. Oradell had finally decided he didn't know. Her mother was an Italian, although born in West Fork. She had been born after Oradell's Italian grandfather got blown up in the West Fork Mine Explosion. Then Oradell's Italian grandmother died, and then Oradell's mother, a little orphan baby, was boarded out with someone, and she herself died too early for Oradell to ask questions. Oradell sometimes wished she had some Italian relatives who knew who she was and grew vegetables and made their own wine.

So that morning she saw how little difference there was between Shacky Hill and Mud Street.

At the bottom, she saw the Downtown, which in those days had the Rialto movie house and a feed store and Miller's Department Store as well as the Company Store with its brick pillared front porch. At the gas station, you could choose to go across the river or up to the mine. Near the river, the houses were a little larger and a little better made, and most of the Americans thought they were just about that much better than the foreigners. At least, that's how Consolidation Coal Company treated them. One row of American houses, the one where Grace Howard lived, had a boardwalk and a view of the river and the play grounds on the bottom.

The company had made an effort to do things nice in West Fork. They had put in those swings and the baseball diamond and the boardwalk in front of Grace's house. They had given a plaque to the High School, and they built a really fine house on the West Side for the mine Supervisor.

The West Side was, of course, where Talkingtons lived, where Oradell was going to get adopted. She crossed over the river, and climbed up the steep brick street past the school, crossed the street car tracks and Route 19 and finally climbed again to the big brick and stone houses where the cream floated on top of the skim.

Oradell was pretty tired by the time she started up the steps to the Talkingtons. The steps had several landings, and she found out later that almost no one ever used the steps. People always took the more gradual driveway. She sat down on one of the landings, and looked back where she had come from, saw the whole thing again from this side: road, street car, river, and town. Hills humped around it all. She saw too much, more than she could understand. Too much! she thought, and a lonely hole opened up in her stomach, and she started to cry, just sobbed away for a long time with her pillow case full of blankets and underwear and skirts pressed against her middle.

Oradell wasn't a crier, but this day, not knowing if her dad would ever come back, and suddenly seeing the whole town like that, she had a feeling that she was missing something she needed. That she might not ever get it.

She cried herself out, until the heat of walking and climbing had dissipated and she started shivering in her cotton dress. A street car trundled past, and some boys were playing an imaginary game of baseball with no equipment outside the Trolley Stop hot dog stand. A Ford roadster backfired, and a dog was barking all the way over on the baseball diamond on the East Side. She picked out Grace Howard's roof and the Company store and the Rialto. Behind everything, hills, yellowish brown fields, reddish tree tips.

"Daddy should of took me with him," she said. "I would of gone if he'd only askt."

She climbed the rest of the steps, and sat down again on the stone porch, the cold coming right through her dress and underpants. She could hear Mrs. Talkington on the phone inside, but she didn't go in. After a while, Sarah Ellen came along the side of the house. She didn't see Oradell, so Oradell said "Boo," and Sarah Ellen screamed, and Oradell laughed and felt better.

Sarah Ellen took her inside and introduced her to the new baby, no different from any other baby Oradell had seen. Grace Howard's new baby had a wee-wee and this one had a crack, but they both were toothless with the tiniest fingernails in the world.

Oradell was much more interested in the house: spacious with highly polished wood floors, carpets, big chairs with fresh slipcovers for spring and lace curtains and a new floor model Zenith Radi-organ with a walnut finish cabinet. Oradell got her own little room with a lavender chenille bedspread. Between Oradell's room and Sarah Ellen's was the bathroom, which was probably Oradell's favorite place in the whole house. It was as big as a bedroom, with a free standing lion-footed bathtub and a porcelain sink that Oradell and Sarah Ellen needed a stool to use, and a huge commode with a wooden seat.

"I'd just as leave sleep in here," said Oradell, not really planning a joke, but when Sarah Ellen laughed, she made the most of it and climbed in the tub and pretended to snore. Then Sarah Ellen climbed in too and they pretended the tub was flying them to a movie set in Hollywood, and they had a long discussion about which movie and which leading man.

All in all, getting adopted went pretty well that afternoon. They had a snack of mayonnaise and sugar sandwiches, and Mrs. Talkington went downtown to the beauty parlor, and Oradell and Sarah Ellen played with the baby.

It was dinner time when Oradell began to have the strange feeling again. It was probably a kind of homesickness, because this was going to be the first time she had ever slept anywhere but on Shacky Hill. Some people, like Mrs. Talkington, saw Oradell's life as disorganized and shockingly unsupervised: Oradell always the last child playing outside in the dark, Oradell cooking for her father, or else they didn't cook at all and he just brought home hunks of cheese and baloney and Nehi orange from the Company store. But Oradell had always slept at home, except for those two nights at the Pierces'.

Mrs. Talkington explained that they ate in the dining room on Saturday night and Sunday dinner. Sarah Ellen and Oradell set the table, and Oradell, for all of her cutting up and joking, paid close attention to how the fork went next to the folded napkin with the crocheted corners, and the spoon outside the knife. Oradell always felt through her whole life that the one thing she knew was the rules for how to set a table, and she learned them from Sarah Ellen Talkington.

Even Mrs. Talkington's cool eye looking her over
and insisting that she have a more thorough wash was
okay. She was used to women dragging her off the street
and checking her for lice or giving her a fresh tooth-
brush and comb.

But by the time they finally sat down at the table—
with darkness outside and the electrified chandelier and
a little music playing elegantly from the Zenith, Oradell
felt that everything was like a picture, but she herself
was not in it. There was Mr. Talkington with his broad
shoulders and glittery glasses, and Sarah Ellen quiet
and light colored like him, and Mrs. Talkington with
her dark hair and cold fish-eye. And Oradell felt silence
falling even as the Talkingtons said this and that: a
bronze-aired spaciousness that was the distance between each of them.

Oradell remembered that she wasn't going to go
home, that she was going to have to pee in the big commode in the bathroom as big as the shack almost and
then go to bed in that room all by herself. There was a
kind of heavy trouble suspended over her head, and
she had the feeling it would be best not to look up.

So she concentrated on the mashed potatoes au gra-
tin. She didn't know yet that you took a little of everything. When she cooked something as good as mashed
potatoes with cheese on top, she and her father always
sat right down and ate till there was none left.

The baby started to cry.

Mrs. Talkington immediately pulled out a hanky
and pressed it to her right temple. "I was so hoping for
a quiet dinner," she murmured. "Oradell?"

Oradell put about a fourth of the potatoes on her
plate, scrupulously leaving enough for each of the

others. She was paying attention to her dividing when Mrs. Talkington said her name. Mrs. Talkington repeated: "Oradell? The baby?"

Oradell didn't get it. She didn't particularly like the sound of babies screeching, but she knew that was what they did. She didn't see any connection to herself.

Mrs. Talkington started to cry. "Nothing is going right," she sobbed. "Nothing, nothing!!"

Oradell was shocked by that too. She had no idea that someone as big and cold as Mrs. Talkington had feelings.

Sarah Ellen and her father immediately leaped up. "I'll get the baby!" they both said.

And it was just Oradell and Mrs. Talkington left at the table. Oradell staring at her potatoes, aware that she had better not eat.

Mrs. Talkington drew back her head. "I was hoping you'd pitch in and help without being told, Oradell. That was my hope. I fully intended to treat you like part of the family, but you have to be willing to pitch in and help."

Oradell said, "I set the table and peeled the potatoes and I sliced the bread." She smelled a challenge; it both was and wasn't like when a kid in the school yard called her dad a drunk.

They came back with the baby, Sarah Ellen holding it in its little blanket and crocheted cap, Mr. Talkington hovering behind.

"Give me my child!" cried Mrs. Talkington. "Give me my baby!"

And the two of them ran over and handed over the baby, even though it had been perfectly happy with Sarah Ellen. Oradell saw now how things were here:

35

Mrs. Talkington told everyone what to do. It wasn't like Grace Howard who just did things, and her big girls just did things, and the boys and Mr. Howard. Sometimes Grace yelled that something was boiling over or Where did they think they were going with the dishes still undried? But it was different from Mrs. Talkington crying Give Me My Child! Part of Oradell's homesickness became a feeling that she couldn't stay here.

It passed through her mind: It's either her or me.

She lay awake deep into the night being afraid of things she had never been afraid of before. Here, she almost fell asleep then jerked awake certain that someone was coming through the window to get her. She listened to every creak and heard a whole platoon of bad men marching upstairs and down the hall. Ghosts flushed the toilets. A wolf howled about death, but that turned into the baby crying again.

She lived for a month at Talkingtons, doing her best to stay out of Mrs. Talkington's way so there wouldn't be trouble. The baby was okay, and Sarah Ellen wanted to take care of it most of the time anyhow. But all along, she had this feeling that if she didn't get away soon, she would either collapse on her emptiness or else get in a terrible fight.

Then, one warm spring evening with the sidewalks and grass wet from a rain, just after dinner, her father knocked on the door at Talkingtons, a big cut healing on his cheek, and his hat low over his eyes, but with a clean shirt and pants.

Oradell squealed and gave him a big hug, and packed her things as fast as she could back into the old pillow case, and then ran down to ask if she should strip her sheets off the bed.

Mr. Talkington answered, "You've been our guest, Oradell. You leave the sheets."

And Mrs. Talkington said, "I had thought we might adopt you, Oradell."

And Oradell, full of unreasoning joy, cried, "You can't! I'm a Riley!"

And hurried off into the night with her father.

Even though she'd eaten a big dinner with the Talkingtons, she let him buy her a hot dog at the Trolley Stop, and she chattered about the Talkingtons and their bathroom and their electric waffle iron and the Radi-organ and the washing machine and how she'd had to iron the crocheted napkins, and how everyone had a special chair for sitting in front of the radio and listening to *Burns and Allen* and *Fibber Magee and Molly*.

Her father said, "I guess you'd rather live with those Talkingtons."

"Not me!" cried Oradell. "No sirree bob!"

But while it was true she was glad to be home, it was also true that she suddenly saw the shack in a different way—saw that the sink was crusty with old dirt and rust, that the outhouse needed lime. And also true that she would not soon forget how she had seen all of West Fork in order, and that she knew now she could sleep in a different house. Something had changed in Oradell, and she kept her eyes open for what was coming next.

- 4 -

On their second day at sea, well out into the Pacific and steaming down the coast toward the Panama Canal, Oradell sat in the small bar next to the dining room. She was wearing one of her short sleeved jackets made out of all kinds of colorful metal bits. She liked to dress up for cocktail hour, and this was her favorite of all the bars on the *Golden Argonaut*. It had plate glass walls and doors onto the main corridor and exactly four small glass-and-brass tables. She sipped Tanqueray on ice and talked to Stavros. She hadn't seen a lot of him today because of the extra work he was doing.

She said, "This Bill Weston at my table is going to wear holes in Jaime's shoe leather. I can see he's going to be the type that considers it a personal insult from Jaime if there's a smudge on his glass or if his lamb chop ain't hot enough. His wife is barely fifty and I swear to God she's had at least two lifts already. I swear to you! Multiple face lifts."

Stavros was making sure he had everything ready for the dinner rush: silver bowls of olives, miniature onions, shaved lemon. "How do you know if a lady has more than one facelifts, Mrs. Oradell?"

"I'm telling you, Stavros, I *know*! It's all in the eyes." She was making this up as she went along. It made her feel good to make it up: this is what you can do when you are old and free or young and wild. At the moment, she felt young and wild. The middle of her life, the hard part, had fallen away. "There are these little lines in the corner of the eyes, not wrinkles, but little lines like you pulled the wrinkles tight and tried to erase them, but the marks are still there. Like explosion lines in the funny papers? You know what I mean, Stavros?"

He wasn't listening, he was working. That was okay. She was happy at her little table. She had her fingers cupped around her goblet of iced gin, the rings on her fingers all colors of gem stones, amethyst, topaz, her little silver pinky ring with the red stone. The air had a density she liked, cool, but also close and moist because of the late afternoon sun boring in.

She sighed happily. "Filthy rich bitch."

"You're filthy rich, too, Mrs. Oradell."

"You hope I am. You're still hoping I'll set you up with a restaurant. I tell you flat out I don't help nobody, but you still hope. I can be a bitch too, you know." She shook her ice against the glass. "I was older than that Weston woman when I met Morris, and I never had no face lifts, either. Morris said, 'What do I want with a little pretty kid like my granddaughter? What do I want with a woman who's going to be winking over my shoulder at the boys?' Morris calculated to the penny. I don't mean he was tight, but he always wanted value for his dollar. He wanted to know how I was spending it, too. I used to take him shopping with me just so I didn't have to report back. He had a driver and not a limousine but a big old top-of-the-line Buick. I took Morris and Frank the driver with me to the grocery store, to the shoe store. Everywhere. Morris got a kick out of it. I'd say, 'Let's go, Morris, we need a quart of milk.' I dragged him all over goddam New York City, and he just laughed as long as we got good prices. We laid it out every day, all over town. Lower East side for dried fruit, catch a sale at Macy's, back uptown to Zabar's for coffee and lox, downtown for lunch in Chinatown. Frank double-parked or went around the block. We had a good time."

Stavros said, "I bet you were good looking when Mr. Morris married you, Mrs. Oradell, because you're still good looking."

"It would have been nice if I'd had the money when I was young and had something worth decorating with all this expensive junk. But I'm not complaining." She drank a little more, felt the silvery settling that came with a few drinks. Such a clean drink, gin. She used to drink sweet ones: Cuba libres and Mai Tais and whiskey sours. Too bad you don't live forever, how much you learn all the time. "Tell me something, Stavros, you know a lot about ships. Is it more of a problem for the captain if a person drops dead in their room or falls over into the ocean?"

"The drowning, Mrs. Oradell. The drowning would be much harder to explain. Especially if there's no body."

"I always liked the idea of slipping off in the water. Salt water and the waves. I had this dream last night where I was floating up to my neck in the ocean with my legs hanging down like a goddam jelly fish. I was watching the ship go away and the sun go down."

"You don't want to die yet, Mrs. Oradell."

"No, I don't want to die yet, but it was a very peaceful dream. It was nice, in that dream, not to be afraid of it."

Stavros stopped lining up glasses and looked directly at her with his large calm eyes. Very softly, he said, "Did I tell you that Mr. Reese from the Company fired Demetrios and the little short boy in housekeeping the day before this cruise? He did it himself, Captain had no say."

"That's a damn shame. I wondered where those boys were."

"They moved one of the casino girls to the Agora Shop. They got rid of Maria."

"Not Maria the beautician, I saw her a day or two ago."

"No, Maria in the Agora Shop."

"Well that's a damn shame too! What's going on? They just gave her a pink slip and said good-bye? Don't you people have a union?" Oradell herself had worked off the books as often as not, but she was always on the union side. Mike had talked union, all day everyday, Mike Brown and the brotherhood of man. She said, "Somebody ought to go talk to the Captain."

Stavros went back to work. "The Captain he don't say much this cruise. Mr. Reese does the talking."

"I'm not complaining," said Oradell. "The *Golden Argonaut* is the still best ship I ever rode, and I rode on the best. You know me."

"It's just changes. Nobody likes changes. New people come in, they make changes." He opened his hands. "Mr. Reese is closing this down too."

When Stavros said Closing this down, she thought for a moment that he meant everything, the whole ship, where she could sleep all night, with the tiny casino, with her starboard-side table and the deep blue ocean.

"Close down what?"

"This bar," said Stavros.

"This one? Why would they close down this one?"

"They count how many people use everything. The Sunset Bar has the grill, people dance at the Sirens Lounge. But this bar, nobody much comes here, and they want me back in the dining room at dinner. So I'm not even suppose to be here. But I said, You got to give me time to break the news to Mrs. Oradell."

"Where am I going to have my drink before dinner?"

Stavros brought her another gin. "Sunset Bar is nice."

"It's too windy back there! It's half a mile from my stateroom to the Sunset Bar! I can't get relaxed for dinner without you, Stavros. And where are the boys going to get our refills during dinner?"

Stavros glanced from side to side as if there might be a spy around. "They have the wine in the dining room, but the boys got to run back to the Sirens or the Sunset every time somebody wants a cocktail."

"Well that's the stupidest waste of energy I ever heard of! I'm telling you, you people need a union!" Mike Brown was suddenly with her. It was as if he were sitting at the table with her with his big grin momentarily clouded over. She and Mike shook admonishing fingers at Stavros. "You think unions are old fashioned? You think it's old fashioned to have people stand up for their rights and take care of each other? When I was growing up in West Fork, the United Mineworkers, they knew how to take care of their people!"

"Working on a ship is nicer than mineworkers."

She shook her head, looked around her little bar. "Well that's a dirty shame, Stavros."

"You go back to the Sunset Bar," he said. "You get some nice fresh ocean air. I'll send you an escort. I got it all planned for you, Mrs. Oradell."

She let Stavros take care of things, but she thought: It's a damn shame. She felt small and deserted, like the little girl on the steps in front of Talkingtons' house with her underwear in a pillowcase.

The next afternoon at five o'clock, Nikko with his dark curly hair and better-than-average English knocked on her door. Oradell had always turned down suggestions from Stavros that she have Nikko up some night. His curly hair and height reminded her of Lance, although Nikko was skinny, and Lance had always been heavy set.

He offered her his arm, and they started slowly down the corridor. "You'll like the Sunset Bar, Mrs. Oradell," he said.

"I know the Sunset Bar better than you," she said. "I've been riding the *Golden Argonaut* for six years! I used to go over there all the time, before the kids started to hang out there, the chorus kids and the casino girls. It got crowded." What she didn't say was that she had also begun to dread the walk a couple of cruises ago. It was all the way aft, and then you had to walk back to the dining room for dinner. "Besides, it's too windy."

"I'll show you a good spot to sit, Mrs. Oradell. No wind. I'll come every day to get you."

She stopped walking to catch her breath. She reached up and patted his long smooth cheek. He had a big head, a full foot above her. "Every day, five o'clock sharp."

"You got it, Mrs. Oradell."

The corridor seemed long. She teetered, put more weight on his arm. "You boys are going to get worn out coming back here for cocktails during dinner. I swear, this man Reese is penny wise and pound foolish. Maybe he's just straight up foolish—" And suddenly realized she had no air, could not talk and walk both.

Nikko slowed down.

The corridor began to shimmer and undulate as if it had no top or bottom or end. What is this? she thought. She wasn't going to be able to do this every day, not if she had to look at this undulation. Doors in the corridor opened and closed.

She whispered, "Let's take a break, Nikko."

He had the sparkliest eyes, a little boy's face up there. "You want me to carry you?"

For a moment, Nikko too wavered in her sight, but he came back. "Not yet," she said. "I'm just out of shape. I'm a tough old bird, Nikko." She leaned both hands on his arm.

Nikko was in no hurry. She liked it that he was young and not in a hurry. "Have you ever been in love, Nikko?"

"Every time I meet a lady."

"Married yet?"

"Not me. I'm the only one, all the boys, Stavros, Jaime, all of them—married! Worried about money all the time, worried about kids. Not me, I'm too smart to get a wife. I spend my money!"

"Yeah, you're right, Nikko. Nobody is going to take care of you but yourself. I know, I've had, and I've not had."

"And having is better, right, Mrs. Oradell?"

"You know it, sweetheart."

She could see the corridor again, the entrance to the Sirens Lounge ahead, the door to the rear deck beyond. They walked on. The Weston girl was out on the deck. "Look there," said Oradell. "What do you think of that one? She's at my table?"

"We all notice *her*."

"She's a hot little number."

"No fooling around with the passengers, Mrs. Oradell."

They walked slowly out into the damp wind. "How are you going to run down here every time someone wants their drink freshened?"

"It's not so far."

"Not so far to you." They made it outside, into the wind. "Get me a good view of the ocean now," she told him. "Put the chair next to the rear rail."

"It's windy there."

"I love wind in my hair." You could look down at the crew deck and watch the boys playing dominoes next to big coils of rope.

Nikko tucked a cotton blanket around her, and she had a whiff of his healthy young body odor. Europeans weren't so eager to shower all the time and scrub off their body odors like Americans.

"*Tan piss* for the Americans, eh, Nikko?" she said, when he came back with her drink. Morris liked her fake French and Spanish, and he taught her some nice chewy Yiddish. She could even make the odd pleasantry in Greek and Italian: *Efharisto. Vagia al'inferno.* I've had some life, she thought. I've seen it all.

"You okay, Mrs. Oradell?"

"I'm fine, honey, go on back to work. I'll just sit here and enjoy the breeze."

If she was too tired to get back to dinner, she'd have a sandwich out here. That's what it was all about, wasn't it? To do as you pleased? It was her favorite hour, with the stiff breeze and the intense colors. Silly flying fish plunging through the rainbows as the ship's wake broke up the whitecaps.

Nikko grinned and made a long humorous bow to Tracy Weston standing at the rail. His long body swooped down, down, and down again. Tracy lifted her head and stared at him over her nose. The bartender tipped his cocktail shaker in Oradell's direction, and she waved. Down below, the domino players waved at her too. Well, thought Oradell, watching Tracy Weston stroll restlessly along the rail, I'm glad I came out today.

A half-level above, the chorus kids were eating early because they had the show every night. Two girls and two boys in khaki shorts. Nice plain faced kids, too thin, but they looked good when they put on their make-up and little spangly costumes. She didn't go to the floor shows much anymore. Her first few cruises, she had done everything: manicure, sauna, casino, massage. You pick and choose, she thought. The doors in the corridor start to close on you.

They had swung far out into the ocean, away from the jungle shores of Central America, making their leisurely loop toward the Panama Canal. The sun was behind them now, the water slick with purple and orange light, the wake swollen and silver. She closed her eyes on the vastness, felt the vibrations of the ship and the damp, implacable wind.

She thought, I've had a goddam interesting life, to tell the truth. She opened her eyes, looking for someone to tell.

The sun was preparing its silent trick of dropping off the edge of the ocean. She spotted a big sea bird, enormous, the kind you only see one at a time, far from land, floating on the air currents. It rotated its head from time to time but never seemed to flap its wings.

Tracy Weston leaned on the rail to her left, also looking at the bird. Hair twisted up on top tonight, tendrils on her neck, long white skirt taut over her precious sharp butt.

"Look at that bird, will you!" said Oradell. "Did you ever see one of those before? I clocked one of them once, twenty two minutes before it flapped its wings."

"It's called a jaeger," said Tracy.

"Oho, a bird watcher."

"At one time I thought of becoming a marine biologist."

"Good for you. You do it, honey. I wish I had stayed in school. I don't think I would have gone in for science, though. I study people."

"You could have been a sociologist or anthropologist."

Oradell felt lucky again: she had wanted a little company, and here it was. "Do you dress like a bride on purpose, honey?"

"White is the family color. It shows off our tans. Also, it makes everyone think I'm a virgin." She glanced at Oradell. "Whether or not I am."

"So now you're going to tell me how nobody your age is a virgin anymore, right?" There was a stir of laughter up above among the chorus kids. Oradell said, "You ought to go talk to them. They pretend they're passengers."

"I'm not looking for someone to hang out with. Just because I'm a teenager doesn't mean I have to be with other kids all the time."

"But you're bored. Being bored is a big mistake, that's what my late husband Morris Greengold used to say. You'll die early if you're bored."

"You don't understand. Boredom is *me*. That's why we're on this stupid cruise. My mom would rather be home playing tennis and Daddy would rather be making deals, but they pulled me out of school because I was bored. I'm supposed to be making top grades so I could apply to all the fantastic colleges, but it looked like I was going to fail everything, so we're pretending I'm sick."

"How about if I fix you up with a boyfriend? That'll give you something to do. I saw you looking at Nikko."

"Who's Nikko?"

"Don't stick up your nose. I saw you looking at each other. The waiter. He's a real fine young man. No wife, no kids. Are you too good for a waiter?"

"It's got nothing to do with waiters! He's too tall."

"Isn't that what girls want, tall dark and handsome?"

"Not me. I like men my size or smaller. It's an eccentricity of mine."

"Eccentricity," said Oradell. One of the other waiters hurried by. "Look at that one running. Starting tonight, the waiters have to come all the way back here for drink refills during dinner. They used to be able to go to the little bar next to the dining room, but they're closing it."

"Why would they do that?"

"It's the same old reason. Somebody thinks they'll get an advantage this way. But you can bet it won't be the working people." She paused, gave Tracy a chance to speak or sidle away, and when she didn't, went on. "Us passengers on these cruises are parasites, honey.

I don't suppose you are, yet, but you will be soon. People are better when they're working than when they sit around waiting to be entertained. The chorus line kids are okay, too. My son did that one year, you know, worked on a ship. Don't worry, I wouldn't try to fix you up with my son. He's much too old for you and wouldn't be interested, anyhow. He isn't into girls. When he did his gig, they got complaints from some Bible Belters who didn't like female impersonators."

Tracy's eyes got wide.

"*That* doesn't bore you, does it? He didn't do it very long. He's really more of a producer than a performer. But he's the one who said, Try a cruise, Ma, you'll like it. He was right, too."

"Was that his father?"

"Who?"

"Your husband who died."

"Morris? My God no, honey. Morris couldn't stand Lance. One of the things I had to do was to keep Lance away from Morris. Morris was a bastard in a lot of ways."

Tracy looked younger and younger. "You mean you agreed to stay away from your own son to please your husband?"

"Honey, it was *much* more mercenary than that. Morris told me flat out he wouldn't leave me any money if he ever had to look at my son the faggot again."

"How could you let him say that!"

"Strictly business." Tracy was so horrified that Oradell added, "Lance knew all about it. I didn't have to stop seeing him, it was just that Morris didn't want to see him. I used to take Lance out to lunch once a week, on Morris's charge card, any place my baby chose, so he studied the papers to find out which restaurant was charging the most. Lance got a trust fund and an apartment out of it, and he'll get a lot more when I go. But I'm glad you think it's terrible, sweetheart. Having money gives you the luxury to be self-righteous."

Tracy said, "My family is not rich."

"I'm not rich either, compared to John Paul Getty or whoever is top dollar dog this week, but you and I, sweetie, we're in a different financial bracket from those boys down there playing dominoes."

Tracy was silent, then said, "Oh, I hate money."

"Don't show your ignorance."

"I do. I hate money. But I'm not self-righteous. Actually, I strive for moral turpitude."

"I bet you do good on your vocabulary tests, too."

"I don't take tests," said Tracy. "I refuse to take the SAT's. It's a boring farce."

"See, that's the proof you've got money! Only the rich do as they please. I'm just saying the difference between you and me is I've been poor, so I know what that's like. I've done whatever I had to do to feed myself and Lance, and you never did. That's all."

"You're marginalizing me," said Tracy. "Maybe someone once told you that you didn't count because you were poor, and that was wrong, but it's wrong to tell me I don't count because I've never been poor."

Oradell liked Tracy. She liked the way the girl grabbed a bite of air so she could talk fast and make her point. Dumb as a post about life, of course, but Oradell didn't hold that against her. It was part of being young. Another time, she'd tell Tracy the story of how she once turned two tricks. That wouldn't bore her either. "Look," said Oradell. "The sun's going."

Tracy said, "Do you think it would be good for me to have an affair or fall in love?"

50

It was time for dinner, and Oradell wanted another gin. "People don't generally pick and choose about falling in love. It just happens."

Tracy said, "I intend to decide everything."

"You can do that maybe for a while, because you're beautiful." Tracy tossed her hair in annoyance, but Oradell added, "Don't worry, it won't last. It's only youth. If you want to stay beautiful, you have to make that your career."

"I don't intend to get old," said Tracy. "I mean, I don't have anything against old people. What I mean is, I'll do a few things until I get too bored, and then, well. You know." She fixed her fox-colored eyes out on the jaeger, still floating. "The one thing I'm sure of is that I'll do something first that isn't boring."

"Yeah, good. More power to you, honey." Oradell did a good deed; she held back the cynical crap about how everyone when they're fifteen feels like they can do something big. Instead, she asked her, "Want to hear what I think a good death would be? A good death would be like that big bird, floating and floating and not going anywhere for a long time and then getting smaller until you're a dot, and then, over and out."

Tracy looked at the bird. "Your generation is supposed to tell me how great youth is, and how I've got my whole life in front of me."

"No, we're supposed to tell you how you'll change and be like us in a few years. Besides, I'm a selfish old gal, honey. I'm not thinking about you at all. I'm thinking about me. I'm getting myself ready for the Big Check-Out, which I hope don't come for a long time, but it will come. One of these days the jaeger is going to come and float over me, and I'll watch it till I don't hear anything else and I'm real calm, and then I'll say, 'Take me Jesus,' and I'll be off."

"Are you religious?" Tracy sounded disappointed.

"No, no. It's just the way you go off, down where I come from. You shout for Jesus." She was suddenly tired. She had to face the walk back down the corridor. "Is it time for dinner?"

"I guess. I'm not very much into eating."

"Would you mind walking me back, honey? I do better if I have someone to walk with me." When Tracy looked frightened, she added, "It isn't catching, honey, what I've got."

"I'm not afraid!"

"I can get Nikko if you don't want to."

"No, no, I like to help."

Oradell did another good deed and held back from saying that sounded more like altruism than moral turpitude. Instead, she asked, "So, what about it? Do you want to get fixed up with Nikko?"

Tracy gave the biggest smile Oradell had seen yet. "God, my parents would go bananas if I went out with one of the waiters."

- 5 -

*O*radell's two tricks were not successful. The last one was when she was getting together a stash of money to run away from Harry, but she lost her temper and walked out without collecting. The other time was one of the reasons she decided to leave Harry. They'd been out of money and drinking like Polkville. She went up to their room to check on Lance, who was about two years old and restless with a fever, and she was getting sick herself, although she thought she was just dizzy from drinking Mai Tais. This was Las Vegas in the late 40's, just as it was starting to take off, big business for organized crime. In those days, the hotels didn't have air conditioning, so it wasn't easy to tell how hot the baby was.

She was falling asleep curled up beside Lance, when Harry came in. He had been talking to a guy in the bar, he said. They made a deal. All she had to do was go to the guy's room, have a drink, be nice to him *eckt settera*, as Harry said. You know the routine.

She didn't want to. She'd never done anything like that before, she whined. Harry hated whining: You do it for free behind my back! he said. So do it for money you lazy bitch!

She made him promise to stay with Lance. She usually ended up doing what Harry wanted because she was sick and tired and afraid of Harry, which was really the part she was most ashamed of, in retrospect: being afraid of that loud mouthed pimp with more hair on his chest than brains in his head. She had a hard time finding the guy's room, and when she was finished being nice to him, found out that he had already given the money to Harry. She went rushing back, and of course Harry was long gone, off to have a party with the money she'd earned, and the baby was having the shakes and jerking around like he was dying. Oradell about went crazy, running up and down the halls screaming for a doctor, and finally found one—in the bar where else— but by that time Lance had settled down on his own, and the doctor told her it was just a fever seizure, happened to babies and little kids all the time.

She didn't trust the doctor, but Lance seemed okay. Mainly, that was when it came clear to her that Harry was the enemy. She lived with him a long time after that, and she slept with him and drank with him, but she knew she and he were on different sides. That night, after Lance finally went to sleep, as the liquor was wearing off, she had a vision. It was very clean and sharp with nice colors. She and Lance were driving across the desert towards sunrise, and no Harry. It took her more than two years to save the money, but she held onto that picture in her mind, and it was what got her through.

It helps a lot to have a picture of how the future should be, she thought.

During those years and later, Oradell worked most often as a waitress. It was active and social, and since people take their food seriously, they will generally treat you okay, if you demand it. Also, you get to eat before your shift starts, and a lot of places had cooks who would feed Lance too. Business was on an upswing, high times in Vegas.

So Oradell always said she had nothing against hookers, it was damn hard work, as far as she could tell. And she herself had certainly humped men for other than love: Harry so he wouldn't get nasty; Morris to help him sleep, and so she'd be in his will. But she was a better waitress than whore.

She often wondered how it would have all come out for her if she had not had her picture of the sunrise in her mind, and also her picture of Mike Brown. Mike was her real love, her gold standard. Because of Mike, she had known from the beginning that Harry was second rate, that there was a better way to go. Harry had been a step backwards toward her first lover, Mr. Bob Myers, manager of the Rialto Movie Theater in West Fork, West Virginia.

She was just a kid, still living with her dad, and she went to the Company store looking for a job. Even though she had turned down his offer to adopt her, Mr. Talkington still helped her out, and he suggested she ought to try to get a job at the Rialto because Bessie Burch had just got a job at Hartley's Department Store in Fairmont and was leaving. Mr. Talkington took her over and helped her get the job. He put on his suit jacket, and as they were crossing the street, he said, "Oradell, aren't you supposed to be in school?"

Oradell did what she often did, which was to tell the truth plus something else. "My dad was sick this morning. Also, I had, you know, woman troubles."

That shut up Mr. Talkington. He was a very nice man, and Oradell had observed, during the weeks she lived at his house, that whenever Sarah Ellen or Mrs. Talkington wanted to change the subject, all they had to do was mention menstrual cramps.

It was also true that Oradell's father had had a fall or a fight and was all bruised up, but neither one of those was the real reason she hadn't gone to school. She hadn't gone to school because the pipe that brought water into their house was leaking so bad you couldn't get water in the sink, and Hugh was too drunk to do anything about it, so Oradell hadn't been able to wash herself a blouse. She had spent the morning making biscuits and eating them and then set the rest on a plate near Hugh for when he woke up. She had found some ribbons in a drawer, which inspired her to braid her hair, put on a pair of Hugh's overalls, and came down town looking for a job.

When they got to the Rialto, Mr. Myers was doing paperwork in his office. It was a little room with green shades, just off the lobby, crowded with a pigeon hole desk and a leather couch. Mr. Myers lived with his wife on the West Side, near the Talkingtons, but no one ever saw the wife. Oradell and Sarah Ellen had tried to spy on her one afternoon, hoping for evidence that she really was a drug fiend the way people said, but she never came to the window.

The two men looked her over.

"I don't know," said Mr. Myers. "She looks like a little girl to me." He was staring at her braids and overalls.

She pulled back her shoulders and lifted her chin, trying to make her bust look bigger. In memory, she always thought of Mr. Myers as yellow-colored. His skin was smooth and he was just barely middle-aged, but he moved slowly and stared at you over the rims of his glasses. He was balding and thick in the shoulders and he wore rimless glasses and a sweater with buttons rather than a suit jacket. He and Mr. Talkington sat on the couch and Oradell stood in the doorway.

Mr. Talkington said, "I can vouch for Oradell as a good worker."

"What grade is she in?"

"She's in high school. She was home taking care of her sick father this morning. Over all, she has a fine attendance record, don't you, Oradell? She lived with us, you know, until her father came back. You couldn't ask for a better girl."

"I'd have to put a box in the ticket booth for her to stand on," said Mr. Myers. "She wouldn't even be able to see the customers if I didn't put a box in."

Oradell was getting tired of being stared at. She said, "Bessie Burch has a stool. I can sit on a stool like Bessie, for Godsake."

Slowly, Myers looked at her, then turned back to Mr. Talkington. "Does she cuss a lot? The person in the ticket booth represents my business to the public at large."

Oradell made up her mind in the instant before Mr. Talkington could respond. Bob Myers didn't own the Rialto any more than Mr. Talkington owned the Company Store, so he was just being a bigshot when he talked about "my business," but Oradell decided—standing there in the doorway to the office with the velvet ropes behind her and a cardboard cut-out of Dorothy Lamour in *Typhoon*— that this was where she wanted to work.

So she stepped all the way into the office and said, "Mr. Myers, sir, I'm sorry I took the Lord's name in vain. I apologize. If you'll try me out, just give me a chance, sir, I'll show you what I can do." She was pretty sure these were lines from some movie she had seen in this very Rialto movie theater.

Mr. Myers looked as if Oradell were a cat that had taken upon itself to argue its own case. She often surprised people. Her whole life was like that—floating along in her rowboat, and then suddenly she would grab hold of the oars for a while and row.

"Well," said Myers, "I guess we can give her a try. Come by tomorrow night, and then Saturday and Sunday if it goes okay. But don't wear those overalls."

She walked right up and shook his hand. "You won't regret it, sir," she said. This time she was pretty sure it was Mickey Rooney playing Andy Hardy.

When they got outside, she asked Mr. Talkington if he had some boxes to haul or something she could do at the Store to earn money to buy an outfit for her job. He said, "I'll do better than that, Oradell," and took her to the safe behind his office in the company store and got out an advance on what he paid her father to sweep the store. "You go over to Miller's and get yourself some outfits," he said. "I'll explain to Hugh when he comes in."

Hastily, Oradell said, "He'll be in later this afternoon, I know he will, Mr. Talkington."

"Now don't you go and buy potatoes with this money. You can always get that sort of thing on account.

This money is for you to buy yourself some business type clothes for work."

"Gosh, thanks, Mr. Talkington. Sarah Ellen is so lucky to have you for a dad!"

He got a little color in his cheeks over that, and his lips flicked a little smile. "Nothing flashy now, Oradell. Business clothes."

She went directly across the street to Miller's Department Store which had the same oiled board floors as all the other buildings in town and lady clerks who were members of the actual Miller family. They always walked toward you slowly as soon as you entered and said, "May I help you?" Meaning, you had better be doing more than feasting your eyes on those lavender gloves.

She said to Miss Miller, "Mr. Myers gave me Bessie Burch's job at the Rialto because she got a job at Hartley's, and I have some money to buy clothes." She opened her hand with the bills in it.

Miss Miller did not look directly at the money. She said, "I think you'll need to begin with Foundation Garments." So Oradell started with a bra and girdle. She was a little embarrassed by the condition of her drawers, but Miss Miller was very professional and started bringing out various combinations of skirts and sweater sets to try on over the Foundation Garments. Oradell selected a tan skirt and an olive green sweater set. She also bought a navy blue dress with a white collar, piping, and belt that made her feel like a Private Secretary. They tried on hats, too, but decided she wouldn't need one just to sell tickets, which was too bad, because Oradell thought she looked real cute in one little military-style number.

She was deeply gratified with how trimly the dress fit over her bosom and rump, shaped and contained by the bra and girdle. Miss Miller suggested a pair of brown pumps as most suitable, or possibly brown-with-white spectators, but Oradell asked to try on the red high heels with toes that weren't quite open, but did have little air holes in them. She could see that Miss Miller did not approve of the red shoes, but Oradell measured the disapproval in her eyes against the fact that no one was going to see her feet in the Rialto ticket booth anyhow.

So she bought the red high heels and still had enough left for a pair of nylon stockings.

Miss Miller rang up the purchases. "These nylons," she said. "may be the last we get for a while," she said. "They'll be needing the nylon for parachutes, you know. The war in Europe."

Oradell knew about the war in Europe, but she didn't pay much attention to it. It wasn't till a year later that the United States got into it and everyone got excited. And by that time, Oradell's life had been completely changed.

At school the next day she borrowed make-up from Sarah Ellen and cut her last class to go home and wash her hair, pincurl it, and practice walking in the red shoes. Having a job was better than living with the Talkingtons, she decided. She was going to earn money and get a washing machine and all the hot dogs she wanted and go to the movies for free and take her father on a trip. She had the vague idea that if she could take him to Washington, D.C. or to a baseball game in Pittsburgh or even New York City that everything would come out okay.

She wore her old shoes and carried her new red heels the first night. Bessie Burch's stool worked just fine. Bessie herself was there that evening to show Oradell how you count back from the price of the ticket to what the customer gave you to make change. She showed her the different colored tickets for the different night's shows. At one point, Bessie said, "I used to know your mother, Oradell."

Oradell sometimes thought she remembered a sunny day and a pretty woman squatting down next to her, because she was hungry or crying. But that was all she remembered of her mother. "No," said Oradell, "I didn't know that."

"Well I did," said Bessie, a woman of few words.

And since Oradell never asked her what she knew, she never found out, and that was one of the regrets in her life. If I just hadn't been so damn eager to barrel on ahead, thought Oradell, I might have learned something. But that was the only night she worked with Bessie, so she didn't have another chance.

Bessie left before the last show, and then some boys from high school came by. "That's not Oradell Riley, is it?" said Bud Mazzei, star of varsity football and basketball. "Nah, can't be Oradell Riley."

"It was yesterday and I expect it's gonna be tomorrow, so I guess it is today too."

"My, my, my," said Bud. "Well, well." He had the nicest little squint wrinkles in the corners of his eyes.

Oradell enjoyed the job. Her clothes were brand new and she had figured out how to keep the lipstick in the line of her lips. She had a talent for making change accurately and quickly. She said, "Good evening, and I hope you enjoy the show," to older people and they said she was a nice girl. I'm always going to have a job, she thought. I'm very good at dealing with the Public.

Nothing seemed impossible. She felt so good that she thought if Tyrone Power or George Raft came down off the screen and offered to take her away, she would just say, Gee thanks, but I've decided to stay right here in West Fork, West Virginia. Or maybe, Thank you so very much for the offer, but I've already got a date to-night. She was especially enjoying talking to the boys who came to the movies.

But what happened was not a movie star or a foot-ball star. Bud Mazzei was very cute and he flirted with her, but he already had one steady girl friend and sev-eral others waiting in the wings. What happened was that Mr. Myers began to stand behind her and rub his body against her back.

Mr. Myers was slow and methodical. It took him weeks to begin to approach her. She had washed her sweater and her dress several times already, and the sweaters weren't holding their shape as well as she'd hoped, and the nylons had begun to take on a whitish color. She wasn't discouraged, but she realized she had a lot to learn about keeping up your clothes and flirt-ing. Stiff Johnson, the boy who collected the tickets, kept asking for a date, but she didn't think much of Stiff's dirty jokes.

She had begun to make herself at home in the ticket booth, doing schoolwork, chewing gum. Gum chewing wasn't allowed, so she chewed surreptitiously on slow nights, holding it under the tongue when she became aware of Mr. Myers watching her through the open door of his office. She thought he had seen her chewing the first night he came lumbering across the lobby and stood in the back of her booth watching her. She got mad, but since he didn't say anything, she didn't either. After a while, he lumbered back to the office.

He did this every night for a week, just came and stood in the back of the ticket booth. Then, one rainy night when there weren't more than five people inside for the first show, he came closer. She heard him breathing behind her, and when she actually felt his breath, she jumped and cried, "Mr. Myers you scared me!"

And he said, "Never mind! Sorry! Just go about your work!"

Oradell had no particular fear of men. Grace Howard used to warn her occasionally. "You're getting on in age now, Oradell," she would say. "You have to watch out for men." It never made any sense to her. She had scrapped her way to a draw or better with most of the boys on Mud Street and even with the Polk kids. The only grown men she knew well were her father, who could be loud and rough but never mean, and Mr. Talkington, who was a gentleman and kind-hearted to boot.

So she had no reason to be afraid of Mr. Myers, except that he might fire her. He came back almost every night after that and stood close behind her and breathed hard. She finally asked him, "Mr. Myers, are you okay?"

"Yes, yes," he said, "Please, don't pay any attention to me."

His reflection in the glass was superimposed on her view of the marquee.

About a week later, he leaned against her back for the first time and breathed in her hair. The night after that, he started rubbing. In the booth, for about ten minutes each night. Very gentle, when things were quiet out front. She got used to his warm and soapy smell.

She didn't say anything. It puzzled her, but didn't bother her a lot. It was nothing like the grabbing she had occasionally fended off from boys. It was more like sitting on someone's porch and having a big old house cat come up and purr against your legs, or a hound dog that kept putting its muzzle up your skirt. She had no romantic feelings about Mr. Myers, so she somehow didn't associate what he was doing with sex.

One night he placed a gift-wrapped package on her lap. He didn't stay and rub her, he just put the gift on her and left. It was perfume. She immediately began to dab perfume on the insides of her wrists and behind her ears. The next night, Mr. Myers asked her to come into his office. It was closing time, and Stiff Johnson and the candy counter girl had already left. No one ever saw the projectionist. Stiff said he slept up in the booth half the time, and if he ever did go home, he used the fire escape.

Mr. Myers locked the main doors, and Oradell followed him into his office, curious about what was next. She was not surprised to see a large box from Hartley's Department Store in Fairmont on his desk. It was another gift, a cream colored blouse with a ruffled collar.

"Well that's awful pretty," she said.

"I thought you might alternate it with the sweater set," said Mr. Myers.

She hadn't thought as far as when to wear it. She had only thought: silky, creamy, all those ruffles. She wondered how she was going to wash it in the zinc basin with cold water on Shacky Hill, but her fingers itched to lift it up. She gave Mr. Myers a big smile.

He blinked behind the lenses of his glasses and then took the glasses off and sat down on the leather couch.

He said, "My wife, Oradell. You know, my wife is—
very delicate."

"I never met her," said Oradell, letting just her left
hand slip into the box, feeling the bottom hem of the
blouse, in case there had been grease on some of the
nickels and dimes she'd been handling.

He turned the light off on the desk so that the only
light was what came indirectly from the street lamp
around the closed green shades. He laid his hand on
the couch beside himself. "Won't you sit down,
Oradell?"

Oradell closed the box to make sure the blouse
stayed clean, and sat beside him. She had an idea of
what was coming.

"It's extremely hard for a man," he said in his slow
way, laying a hand on her knee. "Extremely hard for a
man to live without affection."

"I spect so," said Oradell. She wondered if the
blouse was too good to wear to school and decided it
probably was.

"I have found myself deeply, even *irrevocably* attracted to you, Oradell," he said.

She didn't lie and say she found herself attracted
to him, because she didn't, not in the romantic way,
but he didn't seem to expect her to say anything. He
started kissing her. She let him kiss as long as he wanted.
She thought it over while he kissed her. He wasn't a
stranger, and she had gotten used to his odor that sometimes turned slightly fermented but still fresh like a
big batch of biscuits rising. She could imagine getting
hot, losing control with Errol Flynn or Bud Mazzei, but
Mr. Myers was always polite, never rushed, and she
seemed to have plenty of time to think things over.

He had given her the job, he gave her presents. She couldn't see any reason to stop him from putting his hands on her.

She figured he was going to do it to her that night, but after he had kissed her a lot and felt all over her without taking off her clothes, he looked at his watch and said he had to go. It turned out his wife got very nervous if he wasn't home on time to give her her medicine.

It was another week before Mr. Myers did the whole thing, him with his pants off and Oradell down to her slip. To her disgust, it pinched and hurt and made her bleed like a sissy. It wasn't a lot of blood, more like the stains at the end of her period, but Mr. Myers was terribly disturbed and ran around in his boxer shorts bringing towels from his private bathroom and a wet washcloth for her forehead, which she didn't need because she didn't have a headache.

"Lie back," he said, insisting on putting the washcloth on her head. He knelt on the floor and stroked her wrists. "Oh Oradell, I didn't know. My God, I had no idea. I'm so terribly sorry. This wasn't supposed to be like this—I had thought—I assumed—you were more experienced."

"I am experienced," she said.

"Not with this," said Mr. Myers.

Then it hit her. She sat up and let the wet washcloth fall. "Are you saying you thought I was some kind of a whore?"

"No, no, please, Oradell, I don't like that kind of talk—"

The unfairness nearly choked her. "You think just because—just because—" she didn't have the words for what she wanted to say. It came out as, "You think just because I don't have a mother, you know everything about me! Well you don't!"

"Please, please—" He grabbed both of her hands, he tried to press his face into her lap. She got up and tried to get away from him, but he stayed with her, walking on his knees. "You're soft, you're clean! I never guessed—it's all my responsibility! Forgive me—don't leave! Please forgive me!" He was like a character in a movie, but not the hero. "Please please please Oradell," walking on his knees, pulling her to him, hugging his face into her stomach. His voice was muffled. "So unfair, wrong of me—please don't leave me—"

She thought: He's just afraid I won't do it with him again.

He said, "I was your first, Oradell! Oh God, what have I done? I'm a rotten, worthless—turd."

She started giggling. "A what?"

"I'm a big turd!" he cried, and she couldn't stop laughing, struck by the idea of a chunk of shit the size of Mr. Myers floating down the creek. She laughed until he stopped crying and smiled a little himself and wiped up the floor where the washcloth had splashed.

The next day, he brought her a baby blue sweater set from Hartley's plus a gray, fully-lined skirt, a dozen pairs of nylons, a Whitman's Sampler of candy, and a little glass donkey, a dog, a monkey, and an elephant. She liked the glass animals best, but had to keep them out of her father's sight.

The mistake Oradell and Mr. Myers both made was in thinking that no one in West Fork noticed. Since she wasn't in love, Oradell didn't believe anyone would care. It seemed different to Oradell, like getting premiums for buying a certain product. He treated her very politely and always cleaned up afterwards. What she and Mr. Myers did on the couch in his office after the Rialto closed twice a week seemed something unique, interesting to her and him, but she didn't imagine it would be of interest to anyone else.

One evening Mr. Myers was called away early because his wife was sick. He gave the keys to the candy counter girl, but she had a date and passed the keys on to Stiff Johnson, so that at closing time it was just Stiff and Oradell putting out the lights, looking in the bathrooms to make sure no one had left anything.

Stiff said, "She's a hophead, you know."

"Who is?"

"Myers's wife."

Stiff was two years ahead of Oradell in school, but he had none of the appeal of Bud Mazzei and his crowd. He didn't play football or basketball. His Adam's apple moved up and down just at Oradell's eye level.

Stiff leaned on the carpet sweeper and whispered, "Hey, Oradell, since I've got the keys, let's pretend it's *my* office tonight."

"You stay out of Mr. Myers's office," said Oradell, turning off the marquee lights.

Stiff came up behind her and reached his big hands around and grabbed her breasts, put his grimy fingers all over the ruffled cream blouse.

She hit him in the stomach hard with both elbows and turned around to face him with her fists up.

Stiff said, "I guess you like what he's got better than mine?"

She looked him in the eye, recognized the insult,

saw in a flash that they all knew, everyone at the Rialto and probably everyone at the high school too. She gave Stiff her fastest, hardest combination punch, left to the belly, then a right to his jaw with all her weight behind it from below as he was sinking into the Oof of the belly punch.

He sat down on the floor. "Oradell—"

"Take it back!"

He rolled to his side. "Take back what?"

"Take back what you said about me!"

"I take it back—but I didn't say anything!"

"I'm not a whore because I live on Shacky Hill."

"I never said that."

"You did! Apologize!"

"I apologize!"

She stood there, feeling heat rise from her body, looking down at him. He sat up and rubbed his face. He kept glancing up at her, then glancing away. He said, "I bet you're going to get me fired now."

It hadn't occurred to her that there were any ramifications beyond stopping him from insulting her. "I wouldn't do that," she said, then switched into a Sylvia Sidney impersonation. "But you better keep your big mitts off me, buster."

The next day or two, she went back and forth a lot about herself, Mr. Myers, and the world. Who cares? she thought. I took care of Stiff Johnson, and I'll take care of the rest of 'em. But then she thought, I'm not a whore! And, What's a whore anyhow?

She didn't like having a name attached to what she did. She didn't like feeling that people were laughing behind her back, the way they used to about her clothes.

She refused to do it with Mr. Myers for a week or so, and he bought her even more presents and there were tears in his eyes, so she gave in, and then she refused him again for a while, and this went on for a few weeks. She had so many clothes now that she dressed up for school. She knew what the other kids were saying, and some days it made her furious and defiant, and some days, to get up her courage and show she didn't care, she even wore her red high heels to school. Some older boys started asking her out, and she knew why.

She might have become a real little whore. There were a lot of things that could have happened, and that was certainly one of them. Instead, there was a cold snap in the weather, and her father fell asleep drunk in the alley and froze to death. She missed him terribly, stopped going to school, stopped going to work. She put away her good clothes and wore a pair of his overalls and shirts. She drank his whiskey. The Baptists and Methodists were just gearing up to decide what to do about a girl like that when Mike Brown came to town.

- 6 -

*T*racy Weston showed up at Oradell's door at five o'clock the next day instead of Nikko. "Well, well," said Oradell. "A replacement. I guess you've been talking to Nikko. I guess I don't have to fix you up with him after all."

Tracy wrinkled up her nose again. "I just offered to walk you down today. I talked to him for about forty-five seconds."

Yeah right, thought Oradell, especially when they got to the Sunset Bar and Nikko himself settled them in chairs by the rail and took their drink orders. Smiling at Tracy all the while. She looked ostentatiously bored. For the next two days, it was the same: Tracy walked her down, Nikko saved them seats, Tracy turned her head away and pretended to ignore him. He came back repeatedly to freshen Oradell's drink whether she needed it freshened or not.

"I'm here if you need anything, Mrs. Oradell," he said for the fifth time, looking at Tracy.

Tracy tossed her head.

Oradell watched them watching each other for a little while and tried to feel fond and motherly, but was mildly irritated instead. She wasn't in a mood to be a screen for a couple of youngsters to play peek-a-boo around. She had a life too.

After Nikko went back to work, Oradell said, "You know of course he's not supposed to fraternize. You have to go easy on the love stuff."

"Love!" cried Tracy. She seemed to rise up vertically on her lounge chair and flop down. She was wearing her long white skirt again tonight with a flowery halter top. "That coward? I could never love a coward."

Oradell liked the vehemence. They had been moving right along. "Nikko is a coward?"

"He's afraid to, you know, get together with me."

"You're too young anyhow."

"I'm not! I suppose you still think I'm some kind of virgin."

"Are you?"

Tracy looked pleased to be asked. "I'm extremely choosy about who I sleep with," she said.

"You're a virgin," said Oradell.

"I only have sex when I'm in a great passion."

"Ah," said Oradell. "A great passion."

"Which I could never have for someone mainly interested in following rules. Like him, Nikko. What it comes down to is, he's afraid of getting in trouble by being seen with me."

"This is how he makes his living, honey. It isn't his vacation."

Tracy looked pained. "You both think this is a game for me. Well, I'm not playing. I want—I want—to do something." She turned her face away, out to sea where it caught the light.

"Be a scientist," said Oradell.

"There isn't time. Terrorists could kill us at any minute. Someone could blow up the world before I could accomplish anything. Something has to happen now."

"I always wanted to do something," said Oradell.

"You mean when you were young?"

"No," said Oradell, surprising herself, "now."

"But you're already—"

"Already what?"

"I don't mean too old. I just mean, you seem fine the way you are."

Oradell was restless. She was out of the habit of drawing out young girls. Maybe she had never really been in the habit. "Do you want to hear my love story? It started bad, when I was about your age."

"Yes, please," said Tracy, not looking back at the bar to check on Nikko.

Oradell told her the story of Mr. Myers, finishing with: "He bought me with sweaters and blouses, girly. They weren't cheap, but it wouldn't have made any difference."

Tracy's eyes glowed. "That man should have been arrested for child abuse!"

Oradell said, "Oh, he wasn't as bad as all that. It takes two to tango."

"But you were just a baby! I mean, I know what you're going to say—you're going to say I'm only sixteen myself, but things were different when you were young. I mean, no offense, but people were more innocent. Weren't they?"

"People were doing all the same things and worse. They didn't watch it on the television first, but they still did it. And by the way I was pretty happy with the bargain I made, at least for a while."

"You weren't responsible! He was a grown man!"

Oradell was feeling contrary. "You don't have any idea what a person does when they need things."

Tracy tucked her chin back. "You mean like Nikko needs a job."

Oradell hadn't been thinking about Nikko, but she shrugged. "I suppose. Another time I'll tell you about Mike Brown. He's the one I loved."

"Tell me about him now. Did he save you from the sleazeball at the movie theater?"

"I stopped seeing Mr. Myers before I met Mike. But, yeah, I think he saved me. I married him. I married Mike when I was your age."

That impressed Tracy. "Tell me."

"I want my drink freshened."

Tracy took it over to Nikko, who leaned forward, lowered his head toward her, smiling his squint-eyed smile that was so charming and so careful. Tracy was mad at him. Shoved the glass at him, hand on hip. Why did Oradell want to get involved with such mismatched young people anyhow? Tracy all impatience and used to getting her way, Nikko trained to do as he was told. Oradell closed her eyes: the two of them made her tired.

"He was behind on orders," said Tracy, breaking into Oradell's darkness. She had been almost asleep, or at least in a quiet dark place. "Here's your drink."

"Just set it down."

"Okay," said Tracy.

"Okay what?"

"Okay now you can tell me the story."

Oradell almost told her to go away and leave her alone, but the need to tell rose up in her throat. "Well, let me see. My father died, and I broke it off with Myers."

"The sleazeball."

"Yeah, Sleazeball Myers. And then, while I was still figuring out what to do with myself next, Mike Brown showed up in town. He was a labor organizer, a communist—"

"A communist!"

"He never said it in so many words, but he was always going on about Justice and Bosses and the Working Man. He loved to talk about people getting their fair share."

"That doesn't sound like communism to me."

"Back then it was. Mike had this idea that someday the Bosses were going to get thrown out, and he wanted to help do the throwing."

Tracy didn't look sufficiently impressed.

"And he died trying to do it."

"He died!"

"I didn't say the story had a happy ending."

Tracy's face was suddenly full of color and her eyes got huge. "I'd like to have something to die for! Did the Bosses kill him?"

Oradell noted that Tracy picked up the lingo fast. "As best I could tell, the Bosses killed him. It wasn't clear because I was ignorant and didn't know what questions to ask. But I think so. He was secretive about what he did, but the one thing I know for sure is that he died trying to make the world a better place."

The sun pricked out the separate colors in Tracy's hair: reds, yellows, and dark golds. She's a picture, Oradell thought. She sure is a picture.

Tracy said, "You see, things were better when you were young."

"You make it sound like old is the same as dead. I'm still alive! You're going to get me mad, Tracy. I'm alive, and all that shit is still going on. It only looks romantic in retrospect. It's much harder to see it when it's going on. Look at these waiters, like I told you."

Tracy made a face. "The waiters on this ship are perfectly happy. Nikko loves the Company and he loves his job, and he doesn't even want to talk to me because he's too much of a coward to jeopardize his job. He thinks everything is great just the way it is."

"They talk that way because they think that's what we want them to say. He's trying to protect himself from you."

"That's what I mean. He's a coward."

"Think about it, honey, you're dangerous. It may not seem that way to you, but looking at it from the outside, you really are. Especially to Nikko. And it's just the same on this ship as it always is with the bosses and workers. They closed the little bar to save the Company a few bucks—or because that idiot Reese thinks it will save the Company a few bucks—and now these boys have to go running all over the damn ship to get drinks for the passengers. That may not kill them, but it's what you call a speed-up. It's getting more out of them and not giving them anything in return."

"It's not as bad as, like, factories or sweatshops."

Oradell shrugged. Her drink was finally smoothing things out. "I'm not saying it's as bad, I'm just saying what it is." Tracy was right, of course: Nikko was not going to die in a mine explosion like Oradell's grandfather and all those old Italians and Czechs and the little boys who didn't even get counted because they were working alongside their fathers. Why should Oradell care if a bunch of Greeks and Puerto Ricans had to use a little more shoe leather to do their job? Oradell was on vacation.

And it had been clearer when Mike Brown came to West Fork. The working man versus the Bosses. Mike had told her exactly who was who. Not that Mike did her any big favors, not in the long run.

Tracy suddenly cried out, "Oh Oradell! I'm so glad I know you! The first time I saw you—I never met anybody like you. I saw you, and I assumed you were like my parents."

"Well," said Oradell, "to tell you the truth, honey, when you walked into the dining room that first night, I wasn't too impressed with you either. I said to myself, Here comes Baby Bitch."

Tracy started laughing, and Nikko was just coming out from behind the bar. He saw her laughing, and saw the colors in her hair, and the light on her skin, and Oradell could tell he was a goner.

"Teach me what Mike Brown taught you, Oradell," said Tracy.

"That's all over now, honey," said Oradell. "I'm a capitalist now."

Tracy was going to protest, but here came Nikko to see if they needed anything. And Oradell thought, Nikko, if this little girl wants you, you don't have a chance in Hell.

- 7 -

*S*ome would say that Mike Brown didn't save Oradell but only got her in worse trouble, but Oradell said that however badly off he left her, he gave her a gold standard for men and ideals. He gave her a story that she had been carrying around ever since, tucked in a pocket, not paying much attention to it most of the time, but glad to have it. It made sense of the news on t.v. and sometimes even of what happened to her personally.

Mike's story was simple: rich people are natural bullies, and if the people on the bottom would just stick together, the bullies couldn't push them around any more, and it would be a better world for everyone. He told his story in a clipped, exotic accent that she recognized as a city way of talking, maybe New York or Chicago. His name sounded regular American, but she didn't think the regular American in him was the whole story. There were a lot of details she never found out about him.

Her father died in that freeze, and Oradell holed up in the shack. The Battle of Britain was raging on the radios and in the newspapers; FDR had taken the oath of office for his third term, and John L. Lewis of the United Mineworkers was pretty darn unhappy about FDR. Since the United States wasn't in the war yet, Big John was still striking and threatening to strike. That was what Mike came to northern West Virginia for. He was an organizer, a hero like Gary Cooper in *The Westerner*.

After her father's funeral, people brought Oradell a lot of food. She ate as much as she could, and when the potato salad started to go bad, she threw it in the garbage and ate ham. When the ham turned green, she gave the bone to the Polks' dogs and ate stale cake, and when she had finished that, she stood on a chair and reached into the rafters and got down a bottle of her dad's whiskey. She stopped going to school, and she stopped going to work. She didn't want to go back to the Rialto and Mr. Myers, but neither did she want to live with the Talkingtons. She sat around the shack in her overalls reading funny papers and movie magazines and drinking whiskey. The Baptists or Grace Howard would have done something pretty soon. A town like West Fork didn't let a little girl get drunk every day without making an effort to do something. Grace might have saved her if Mike Brown hadn't, but it would have been a different life.

One morning, bored and with a slight buzz on, she realized there was nothing to eat in the house, so she walked barefoot down to the Company Store with cold spring mud oozing up between her toes and numbing her feet. She went into the store and sat down on an empty crate. She was thinking she might ask Mr. Talkington for her father's job sweeping the store.

Mr. Talkington frowned. "Oradell, did you have breakfast?"

She must have looked awful. She shook her head.

He made her a baloney sandwich and gave her a Coke, and she was eating and letting her muddy feet thaw out against the Warm Morning stove when Mike Brown came in.

Mr. Talkington greeted him by name. He was a little bow legged, and he wore loose fitting Levi pants like the miners and a khaki shirt and brogans, but his cap was a black beret, as if he thought he was in France instead of West Virginia. He was dark-eyed and curly-haired with wrinkles in his forehead that reminded Oradell of John Garfield in *They Made Me a Criminal*. She wondered if he was an Italian like her dead grandfather.

He bought a stick of sausage and a quart of milk. He ate standing, alternating gulps of milk with bites of sausage. His way of talking was slow and drifty the way men did in those days, but his words had that foreign sharpness around the edges. After a while, he came over and sat on another crate next to Oradell. "Hello, sis," he said, and went right on talking to Mr. Talkington and the butcher. Mr. Talkington was saying that he didn't understand why the miners weren't happy with their $7.00 a day, which was the best they'd ever gotten.

Mike Brown ran his tongue around inside his teeth and said, "The miners down in the southern part of the state make less. A lot less. The ones up here and the ones down there need to stand up for each other."

From behind the counter, the butcher said, "John L. Lewis is doing what he's doing because he's mad at FDR."

"You may be right about that," said Mike Brown,

"but it's still a big chance for the miners. They know they need us now. They can't have their war without the miners."

Then they talked a little bit about the war in Europe and how the U.S. was sure to get into it, not whether, but when. Then they drifted back to the weather, and Mike finished his milk and sausage and handed the bottle back over the counter. "Well," he said, "I guess I'll be going now. I hope you gents have a real fine day." Mr. Talkington and the butcher wished him a good day too. Oradell followed him out.

She followed him up the street, to the bridge, where he turned up the hill toward the mine portal. Oradell turned up too. At the first curve, there was a building that used to be a store but was boarded up now. He stopped there and lit himself a Pall Mall cigarette. "Are you following me, sis?"

"It's a free country, ain't it?" said Oradell.

Mike propped up his leg on the porch of the boarded up store and leaned on his thigh and smoked. "I don't know," he said. "Do you think it's a free country?"

"I do what I want to," she said, "so I guess I'm free."

"Well now." Mike Brown squatted down suddenly like a man talking to a little child. "Well now, if it's such a free country, how come you don't wear shoes?"

"I have shoes! I have a whole box of shoes. I don't feel like wearing them today."

"And that makes you free?"

She wished he would stand up instead of squatting. She wished he could see her in her red high heels.

"And since you're so free, you're going to trail me up to the mines where I have to talk to some workers?"

"Maybe."

81

"Well, I wish you wouldn't."

She said, "You ain't from around here. You sound like the Bowery Boys."

He burst out laughing, which was his mistake, because Oradell liked the laugh even better than the rest of him. His laugh used his whole body. It made his arms lift up and his cigarette wave around, and his bandy legs bounce. He stood up. "Shouldn't you be in school anyhow, sis?"

"I'm not going to school. My father died."

"I'm sorry to hear that."

"He froze in an alley. He drank himself to death, and my mother died when I was two years old, so I'm on my own."

"You're on your own, are you? You don't look like you take very good care of yourself, Miss On-Your-Own. You're going to get sick with no shoes."

"You can't tell me what to do," said Oradell, already hoping that he would.

"I wouldn't try to," he said. "I'm very sorry about your recent loss, but I have to get a move on. Maybe I'll run into you later today." He tossed his cigarette and glanced up toward the mine. He said, "Listen, sis, seriously now, I got to go to work. I think it's best if you don't follow me up there."

Oradell said, "My granddaddy died in that mine. He died in the Great Explosion of 1908. That's before I was born."

He burst out laughing again. "I'd say so!"

"I'm sixteen!" she cried. "Almost. I've been work-ing since I was little. I'm older than I look."

His mouth twitched. "Yeah, but you sure ain't any cleaner than you look. Listen, I'll tell you what, sis, you leave me alone now, and after I do my work, I'll buy you an ice cream soda. How does that sound?"

"What time?"

"I don't know. Two o'clock. How about two o'clock?"

"Right here?"

"Sure, right here."

"All right," said Oradell, and she sat down on the steps of the abandoned store.

"You're going to wait? You're going to sit there and wait for me?" He walked off, bent over his laugh.

She sat in the sun and cold air for a while rubbing her feet, and little by little, as her brain cleared, she changed her mind. She went home and brushed out her hair and braided it, washed her face, underarms, and crotch, and put on a school skirt.

She had plenty of time to be back at the abandoned store when he came down the hill with some miners. They all saw her sitting there, and one man asked her how she was doing, and she said fine. She trailed behind Mike and the other men. The miners turned up the street where Grace Howard lived, and Mike waved good-bye. Oradell caught up to him, and he said, "Cleaned up, did you? Now, where do you go around here for an ice cream soda?"

"The coffee shop at the Fairmont Hotel," she said. She didn't want to have her soda with Mike Brown in West Fork. School would be out in a few minutes, and Mr. Myers would be going over to the Rialto.

"Fairmont! That's a way up the road! Do you figure I have a car?"

"We could take the street car."

It turned out he did have a car, not much of one,

but they drove to Fairmont and had burgers and milkshakes, and drove around town, and he pointed out how large and prosperous the banks and Hartley's department store were compared to how the miners lived, and that was her first lesson on bosses and workers. They spent the whole afternoon together, and Oradell never wanted it to end.

She didn't inquire that afternoon or ever about his reasons for being with her: whether he felt sorry, or maybe had heard the rumors about her being a baby whore. Oradell never pretended to know what Mike Brown thought, but she knew what she felt when she was in his presence. Whether they were in a restaurant eating hot roast beef sandwiches with mashed potatoes and gravy, or walking into the Lee Movie Theater in Fairmont, or when they were in private and he put his hands on either side of her face and kissed down her forehead and nose, and her whole body seemed to unzip itself—whatever they were doing, he had everything she needed, and she tried to press as close against him as flesh allowed forever.

He sent her back to school, if only so she wouldn't get bothered by the Baptists. Evenings, though, she found him wherever he was, at the United Mineworkers hall or in the rooming house where he stayed, or at the Company Store. Everyone knew about how she was following him, and he kept saying she was getting in the way of him organizing, but then he would laugh and buy her a hot dog at the street car stop. He'd drive her home, and she'd make him come in the house and tell her more about the Bosses, and what was wrong with FDR and even Eleanor Roosevelt, who was a lot more popular than her husband around West Fork.

She cooked him biscuits and made pan gravy, and one Sunday afternoon as he was sitting in his undershirt reading the paper aloud to her while she washed out his work shirt, Grace Howard walked in. This was an amazing event because Grace Howard didn't go out much, not even to church. But she had on her church clothes this day, including a navy blue hat with a veil and painted wood cherries. She stood in the doorway breathing heavy, and she wouldn't sit down. "Now look here. Oradell, the first thing is I don't want to hear a word out of you. I want to talk to this man. Mr. Brown," she said, "I have one question: are you and Oradell engaged?"

Oradell said, "I don't care, Grace."

Grace said, "I told you to shut up, Oradell. I'm talking to him. Are you?"

Mike said, "Please believe me, lady, I don't mean her any harm."

"She's a good girl who has had a hard life, and you're a man, and what I want to know is, are you engaged to be married?"

"No," said Oradell.

Mike looked at Oradell, and he looked around the house. He said, "You know, Mrs. Howard, I'm a man who has to travel."

"I can travel," said Oradell.

Mike explained that his life was to go around and help the miners and other people on the bottom get together so they couldn't be pushed around anymore, and Grace Howard said that sounded real Christian, but if he was such a one to help other people, how come he needed a little girl like Oradell to wash his shirts and make his biscuits. And furthermore, if he didn't marry

Oradell and make it all right for her to wash his shirts and make his biscuits, then Grace was personally going to see to it that he got run out of town.

"You wouldn't!" said Oradell. "I don't give a good goddam what people think!"

Mike and Grace stared into each other's eyes, and then they both stared at Oradell.

"I don't want to get married," said Oradell.

Mike turned back to Grace and said, "All right, Mrs. Howard. Let's me and her get married."

"What if I say no?"

"When?" said Grace. "Because I have to get my husband's blue suit out of the mothballs, and I may just buy me a new hat. We're going to go with you to the County Court House and stand up with you and see that you don't change your mind."

Mike's face broke up in one of his shiny laughs, but not Grace, she wasn't about to laugh until she'd taken care of things.

And she did. On Tuesday morning, they went in Mike's car to the Court House. It was a beautiful June day. Oradell bought a new seersucker dress with a little short white jacket and a white picture hat that was so stylish and big she had to take it off to fit in the car. Mike refused to wear a suit jacket, but he borrowed a tie from Mr. Howard, and he wore it with a clean, pressed work shirt. Afterwards, Grace set out a lunch like a picnic with potato salad and fried chicken, and then Mike moved into the shack with Oradell. On Sundays he fixed the roof, which made Mr. and Mrs. Pierce mad because you shouldn't work on Sunday, so Mike switched to Saturdays out of solidarity with the Pierces because they were colored.

He married her awfully easily. She sometimes thought in later years, when she was mad at him, that maybe the people who whispered that Mike never really married her might have been right. That is, they had certainly gotten married, and he gave her the little silver ring with the red stone and a marriage certificate, and there were witnesses and the wedding lunch, but Mike had a lot of secrets. He appeared and disappeared often. She wondered sometimes later on if he had another name, another life, maybe even other wives. But the truth was, she didn't care. Not then.

I was his goddam puppy dog, she sometimes thought. And then felt mixed up—guilty because she loved him to death, mad because he left her in the lurch.

Later that summer, he got a phone call and told her he was going to have to go up to the anthracite coal fields of Pennsylvania. The UMW strike around West Fork had pretty much petered out, and Oradell was ready to pack up and go with him, but it turned out she was pregnant, and Grace Howard had another little talk with Mike. Mike ended up agreeing with Grace again, against Oradell: a pregnant girl can't go off organizing, they said. She was going to sit in West Fork and get fat while he did his work.

She didn't care that much about the validity of the marriage certificate, but she cared a lot that she had to stay in West Fork when he went. If she had gone with him, if she had had another week, another day, an hour. Sometimes, idly, she tried to figure out what she would trade for another hour with Mike. All her cruises on the *Golden Argonaut*? Probably not for one hour, but she thought she would trade them in for a week.

- 8 -

They were approaching Oradell's least favorite part of the cruise. After four leisurely days of floating out on the Pacific, while everyone made friends and paid attention to one another's stories, they started visiting points of interest. Tomorrow they would pass through the Panama Canal, then visit ports in Panama and Colombia, Venezuela, and Aruba, and finally debark in San Juan. Oradell had announced at several dinners that she didn't do all that shopping shit anymore, but no one cared. She didn't like the long, hot days in port followed by dinners where the other passengers had the fresh experiences to tell.

She was feeling a little disgruntled the evening before the Panama Canal. On the way to dinner from the Sunset Bar, she got breathless again, and Tracy made her sit down and rest in the lounge. They didn't sit long, but it made them late getting into the dining room. There was a high level of noise, people in a mood to celebrate because of the Canal coming up tomorrow. Jaime came past taking long heavy strides, muttering and cursing.

"Take it easy, Jaime," said Oradell. "You're going to end up with apoplexy before I do."

He snarled something along the lines of "I do one good job I don't do six good job," and thundered on.

Now what's that all about? wondered Oradell.

As they passed Goldienails' table, Ilene Blume started to wave. "There they are!" called Ilene. "Tracy's with Oradell, and everything is okay!"

From the expression on Cathy Weston's face, everything was not okay. As Tracy helped Oradell get settled, Cathy said, "Bill, ask Tracy where she was."

Bill Weston was poking at his shrimp cocktail. "Where were you?"

"This is a ship, Daddy. I never left the ship."

"We haven't seen her since before lunch," said Cathy Weston. "She's been hiding from us all afternoon."

Bob Blume cleared his throat. "Ilene, remember when we had a house full of teenagers?"

Ilene said, "Absolutely. I also remember when *I* was a teenager. I was going to divorce my parents."

Stavros came by and lit the tall candle in the flowers of the centerpiece. Bill Weston said, "Where's our waiter? I need cocktail sauce."

"He will be with you shortly, sir," said Stavros. "He is at his other table."

Weston picked up a shrimp and said, "At least they manage to keep the shrimp fresh. How do you suppose they kept them fresh after this many days at sea?"

"Maybe they catch them off the side?" said Ilene.

"Impossible," Weston snapped. "Shrimp are shallow water fish."

"They aren't fish," said Tracy.

"We're taking this trip for her," said Cathy, "God knows it wasn't my idea of a vacation. We thought it might cheer her up—"

"You may address me directly," said Tracy.

"We love you Tracy darling," said Cathy Weston. "Whatever you do or say, we'll always love you."

Bob Blume said, "It's too bad there aren't more young people around."

Tracy said, "They brought me to get me away from kids my age! Right, Mom? She thinks all the kids at my school are heavy metal Satanist cult killers. You know, just your typical California teenagers. And the rest are communists!"

"That's a new one," said Weston.

"I won't say a word," said Cathy. "Whatever I say sets her off. A simple little word from me and off she goes about cult killers and communism."

"We came for this vacation in the middle of a busy period," said Weston. "Lots of deals pending. Planned community for seniors, all first class, medical facility, swimming pools indoor and out. Nine hole golf course. Choice of restaurants. The kind of place a person can go and never leave."

Oradell said, "Where I come from, we call that Heaven." They weren't paying much attention to Oradell. She wondered if she was getting what she paid for this trip.

Bob Blume said, "I just realized, I don't know what flag this ship flies. It flies some flag you wouldn't expect. I think it's the Bahamas."

"Panama," said Weston.

"It's the Bahamas, isn't it?" said Blume. "Ilene?"

"Isn't it Greek? The waiters are mostly Greek, aren't they?"

"There's no connection between the flag they fly and the management of the ship," said Weston. "It's Panamanian. It's the major Panamanian industry, ships flying their flag."

Bored, Oradell looked around the dining room. Reese the Company Man was just coming in the main entrance. He rotated his ugly pale face with its little moustache side to side, scanning for trouble.

Bill Weston said, "Where's the waiter? He was supposed to get me more cocktail sauce and a refill, and he disappeared."

Someone shouted. It was loud enough that the dining room noise died down. Jaime had just come in with a heavily loaded tray.

"There comes my drink," said Bill Weston. "It's about time, too."

Oradell didn't have a great view across the room, but good enough to be pretty sure Jaime was the one who had shouted. Yes, Jaime was shouting again, his voice picking up volume in a way she had heard before. "Hold onto your hats, folks," she said. "I think Jaime's about to blow."

He threw the tray. He didn't just drop it, he spun it in an impressive arc through the air and the glasses and liquids made their own separate arcs. People screamed, ducked, leaped from their chairs. Stavros came running from one direction and Nikko from another, but Jaime outran them, burst through the crash, heading for Reese, who, to give the devil his due, held his ground and raised his fists like an old-fashioned prizefighter.

Oradell was thankful that she still had her distance vision.

Nikko caught hold of Jaime before he could do any damage, but he kept screaming and swinging, and there was more clattering as he kicked a serving cart. Oradell noted that Goldienails screamed with her eyes open so she wouldn't miss anything.

"Watch out, Mr. Reese!" said Oradell. "You don't know my boy Jaime."

Cathy Weston cried, "Bill! Do something!"

Bill Weston threw down his napkin and strode across the dining room.

"Don't *you*," said Ilene Blume to Bob.

The whole room was standing now, except for Oradell. The Blumes, Cathy Weston, Goldienails, the Poodles, Pinkie, Doc Clyde, and Johnny. "They're blocking my view," said Oradell. "Tracy, get up on the chair and tell me what's happening."

Tracy clambered up on her father's chair, and Cathy told her to get down. Tracy said, "Daddy's grabbing that man from the Company!"

"What's Jaime doing?" said Oradell.

"I don't know. I don't see him."

"Did he hit anyone?"

"It looked like he hit that man. The man from the Company. I think he's got a bloody nose."

The disturbance surrounded Oradell like a kind of insulation. The roll basket was directly in front of her, and she was drawn to one small, perfectly round dinner roll with a golden brown crust. She seized it, plunged both thumbs in and broke it open, was gratified by its soft interior. She buttered it and ate. Too bad, she thought, feeling that something was coming to a close: Jaime's career as a waiter, maybe. She drank wine and ate her roll. The other waiters set things back up, asked people to go back to their tables. Bill Weston came back limping.

"Your knee, Bill!" cried Cathy. "You didn't tear the cartilage again, did you?"

He made a pooh pooh gesture and seated himself, looked around the table. "It was nothing," he said. "A troublemaker hit Reese. Can you believe that?"

"It was our waiter, wasn't it?" said Ilene Blume. "My God. Is everyone okay?"

"What happened to Jaime?" Oradell asked.

Bill Weston said, "I think he ran away." He was almost smiling, the most cheerful he'd been all trip: clearly a man who thrived on action.

You could see Reese and Stavros and now the First Mate and the Chief Steward talking together. Doc Clyde was patting Reese on the shoulder. There was no sign of Jaime.

Bill said, "Of course, they'll fire the waiter. I hope they arrest him too."

"Jaime's been on this ship as long as I've been riding it," Oradell told them. "He's a hot head, but he's still a good boy."

Cathy said, "Well, he can't be a very good boy if he goes around punching guests."

"Reese isn't a guest. Reese is a goddam bird dog. Reese is a sniffing nose for the company."

Nikko appeared with a pad and pencil, tiny in his big hands. "Good evening Ladies and Gentlemen. I am Nikko, your waiter for tonight."

"What happened to Jaime?" asked Oradell.

Nikko smiled up at the ceiling lights. "He is—off duty."

"Off duty to hell," said Bill Weston. "Off the pay-roll is where he'd better be."

"So," said Nikko, "for this evening tonight, *I* am your waiter!"

Tracy said, "Did he do that because he had to go too far to get the drinks?"

Cathy rattled her menu. "I want the chicken, but with steamed vegetables. May I have the vegetables steamed?"

"Madame," said Nikko, flashing his smile, bending toward her, "you name it, you got it! Chicken, with vegetables steamed."

"You see!" said Ilene Blume. "Now I call that service. I'd like the trout."

Tracy said, "Did they give you his tables instead of yours, or his tables plus yours?"

Oradell was proud of her little protégée's solidarity. Not bad, she thought. Mike Brown would be proud too.

"They divided up, Miss Tracy. You want another drink, Mrs. Oradell?"

"No, thanks, sweetheart."

Cathy was looking at Nikko. Oradell wondered if she was suspicious because he knew Tracy's name.

"Well I want another drink," said Weston. "I never got the refill on my Chivas Regal. It got spilled on the floor by that crazy Puerto Rican. On the rocks."

Tracy laid down her menu. "Daddy, don't you see? That's the problem. The waiters have to go all the way to the back of the ship to get refills. It isn't fair."

Weston said, "I don't give a goddam. They promise service on this barge, and I want my drink freshened."

"No problem," said Nikko. "Glad to be of service."

"Damn straight."

"I'll just take the rest of your orders," said Nikko,

speaking to all of them, but looking at Tracy. "That way, the kitchen can get started. Then, I am off to get the drink like a flashlight!"

"Like a flash," said Tracy. "Not like a flashlight."

Cathy was definitely watching Nikko and Tracy. Tracy and Nikko were watching each other. Plenty to look at, but Oradell was troubled. She didn't seem to be able to keep a buzz on. Maybe she wasn't drinking enough. Jaime was never meant to wait on people. He was meant to have his own little shop or maybe deliver mail somewhere. Something where he was his own boss or at least worked alone. What would they do to him for punching Reese? They'd fire him of course. But Oradell didn't want to be worrying about Jaime for Godsake. She was on vacation. She was supposed to be enjoying herself. She decided she really needed to drink more, and exercise less. Too much exercise going down to the Sunset every night.

I'm here to do what I want, she thought. I'm on vacation for the rest of my life.

She got up before Nikko came back with Bill Weston's drink. "I'm turning in early," she said. "Tell Nikko I'll order in later if I want something."

"Are you okay?" said Tracy. "Do you want me to come with you?"

"I'm fine," said Oradell. "I don't need any goddam children leading me around."

Tracy looked stricken. Goddam right, thought Oradell, I'm not your granny, and I'm not your friend. She made her way all the way across the dining room without losing her breath.

- 9 -

Mike Brown had told her he'd come back in a week or two, but he was gone three weeks, then five. Oradell hand-sewed flowered curtains for all the windows in the house. She got dressed up and ate Sunday dinner with the Howards, read magazines, and visited Sarah Ellen Talkington. She missed Mike, but wasn't sad. It was a quiet time; the Polks weren't fighting, and the Pierces gave Oradell tomatoes and beans from their garden. She did a lot of sitting on the porch looking alternately at the farms on the back side of the hill and then at the mine tipples on the other side of town. She thought about how she and Mike and this little baby were going to travel all over the world in Mike's car and make everything right for All the People.

On the sweetest Indian summer morning of all she was sitting there in the golden haze when Mr. Talkington's green Nash came up Mud Street. Mr. Talkington was alone in the car, and he pulled it up near her house and got out. He took his time. He had on his suit jacket, and he was holding a little yellow paper. He said, "A telegram came in for you, Mrs. Brown."

It was the first time anyone ever called her Mrs. Brown. She took her bare feet off the porch railing but kept her hands in her lap.

Mr. Talkington said, "It's for you, Oradell." She didn't like the looks of that yellow slip of paper. "You have to read it."

In the next day and a half, a lot of papers got stuck in her face, and she didn't read most of them very well. She didn't read the words of this one either, but it seemed to say that there had been an accident in Kentucky, and she was supposed to call a certain phone number and reverse the charges.

"How come it says Kentucky?"

Mr. Talkington cleared his throat. "Well, Oradell, I think it means Mike— Mr. Brown— I think there was a accident, Oradell. But you better come down to the store and call that number and find out for sure."

"But he ain't in Kentucky," she said. "That's not Mike. Mike was going to Pennsylvania."

She went barefoot into the car. She kept staring at Mr. Talkington's pant leg as they drove down Mud Street. He parked between the store and the gas pumps, and they went up the steps, across the oiled boards of the main room, between the butcher's counter and the cash register and into his office with its ceiling as high as it was wide. He offered her the rolling chair and the telephone.

They accepted Reverse the Charges at the number in Kentucky, and the man she talked to was very polite. He called her Mrs. Brown and explained that they were wiring her a train pass. They were going to meet her at a certain station in Kentucky, he said. They would give her the money and the remains.

Oradell couldn't get her mouth open to say: What money? What remains?

The man told her all she had to do was sign a receipt, and then she could go home. They were very sorry about the accident, but this would be the smoothest way to do things.

She understood that the man talking was named Timothy McClain. He was polite, but he talked fast. He gave instructions, and he didn't answer questions.

"Now is it clear, what you're going to do, Mrs. Brown?" he asked. "Because we'll have someone to meet you when the train gets in. Once you get the ticket and know which train you're on, you have to call back so we can meet you."

She kept nodding her head and forgetting to say Yes.

Finally she managed to say, "Listen here. Mike went to Pennsylvania."

"We want to offer our deepest condolences, Mrs. Brown," said Mr. McClain. "We know this is a difficult time for you."

She said good-bye and hung up the phone and stared at Mr. Talkington. She couldn't answer any of Mr. Talkington's questions, so he called the number back and spoke with Mr. McClain. Oradell stared at the picture of a light house on the wall calendar.

Mr. Talkington got off the phone and said, "I'm real sorry, Oradell. I can't tell you how sorry I am."

"But it's a mistake," she said. "Mike's in Pennsylvania."

"Wherever he went to, Oradell, he ended up in Kentucky. I'm real, real sorry. Mike was a fine man, of his type. I mean, of any type. Just a fine man."

Stupidly, Oradell said, "Oh, it's all right."

When she looked back at her life, Oradell never felt particularly sorry for herself about anything but that trip to Kentucky. She wasn't sorry for herself for having the father she had or about marrying Mike Brown and having the baby. But it still made her want to cry for how they let her get on that train all alone. She had never been more than fifteen miles from West Fork. She didn't know what to wear, what to ask. She was feeling queasy in the stomach. It wasn't just Mr. Talkington either. He called up Grace Howard, and Grace told Oradell she was real sorry about Mike, but Grace didn't stop her from going.

Of course, in defense of Mr. Talkington and Grace, they didn't think the coal company was the enemy the way Mike did. They thought the coal company was being good to her, doing the right thing.

She might have gone to the Union Hall, if she'd been thinking, but she wasn't thinking. Or rather, she was thinking, but she was thinking once she got there, Mike would take care of everything.

Mr. Talkington sent her home to get dressed. He would make sure the ticket got wired in, and he would drive her to the train. She nodded her head, concentrating on how to do what she was told. She walked back up the hill, passing the little house where she thought her mother might have lived. There were huge blue morning glories on a trellis there. Somewhere in the distance was an impact: the whack! of an enormous hammer.

She washed her feet and put on her open-toed red high heels. She didn't have any stockings without runs, so she went bare-legged. She wore the same seersucker dress with the little short sleeved jacket that she got married in, even though the belt rode high over her belly now. At the last minute she remembered to get up on the shelf and take down the red leather pocketbook Mike had bought her to match the shoes. She didn't have anything to go in the pocketbook, though, except fifty cent's worth of change and a lipstick. She forgot her hat, and during the whole trip kept thinking it was a big mistake not to be wearing a hat.

Mr. Talkington came up the hill in the car to get her, and he drove her to Clarksburg so she could catch the westbound train direct. While they were waiting for the train, Oradell said, "I doubt it was really Mike. He said he was going to Pennsylvania."

Mr. Talkington said, "Honey, Mike traveled around quite a bit. I think that Mr. McClain knew who they had." He kept looking over at her. "Are you going to be okay, Oradell? Be sure you get the money, Oradell. Do you understand?"

"Nobody's going to put anything over on me," she said.

"You'll be fine," said Mr. Talkington. "You just act like you're a tough cookie."

He gave her ten dollars and put her on the train. She rode the train in her high heels with her pocketbook on her lap all day. She was afraid to get up to go to the bathroom or to look for something to eat. She was afraid if she moved something would break. Sick with hunger and weariness, she kept dozing into the afternoon, changed trains in Cincinnati, rode into the sunset and the night.

The conductor woke her. "This is where you get off," he said.

It was black outside. Struggling up out of sleep, she asked "What time is it?"

"Two-thirty," he told her, leading her to the end of the car, helping her down. "Don't you have a suitcase? Didn't you bring a suitcase?"

"A.M.?" she said, stepping awkwardly into the cold damp night. Her knees were buckling. "I don't know if this is where I'm going," she said.

The conductor waved, the wall of metal clanked and growled, and pulled away. She didn't even have a sweater. She hobbled a couple of steps back from the moving train. She was on an unsheltered platform, misty in the night, with a sharp smell of unfamiliar vegetation. The mountains were blacker and taller than the ones at home.

She was alone on the platform. Her train chugged, whistled, its rear lights receded and flickered away. For a while the rails hummed, then stopped. She strained her ears. The stillness was thick and cold. Then she began to feel motion again, but it was her knees shaking. She was not conscious of being in danger or frightened, but the knees and then the whole front of her thighs began to shudder. She turned herself around in a circle, looking for something.

There was a building on the other side, and standing apart from it, near the tracks, was some kind of bench with no back rest.

Three men in suits came out of the building and crossed the tracks to Oradell.

Her breath was coming fast and her knees and thighs wouldn't stop shuddering. In her mind her own voice said clearly: *I'm cold as the dickens*. The three men all wore suits with vests. It was hard to see their faces, because the lights were behind them. One was big and fat; one had especially broad shoulders; the smallest one was rumpled and weighed down with a briefcase.

He was the one who removed his hat first, then the other two did. "Mrs. Brown?" he said. "I'm Timothy McClain. We spoke on the telephone." He kept right on talking, whether she answered or not. He was so sorry for her grievous loss. He hoped her trip had been as comfortable as possible, given the circumstances. "Let's cross over to the other side," he said. "The eastbound will be coming along, and we want to put you right back on the train so you can return to your loved ones as soon as possible." He pressed close on one side of her and took her elbow. The man with the big shoulders pressed close on her other side.

They helped her across the tracks and the riprap stones that made her heels slip and sink. The fat one breathed loudly behind them, and they all came to a stop next to the benchlike box. They kept their hats off.

Timothy McClain wished there had been a kinder way to break the news to her. The fat man cleared his throat. "We have some papers for you to sign," said Mr. McClain.

Oradell kept staring at the box. It was too dark to get a good look at it, but she thought she recognized the shape. She said, "Is Mike in that there box?"

"Yes, Mrs. Brown," said Mr. McClain, "I hope you'll accept our deepest condolences."

She finally looked at their faces: Timothy McClain was chubby and had wrinkles in his forehead and needed a shave. The one with the shoulders was good looking and had a toothpick in his teeth. The fat one kept his head up so that his eyes were always hidden from her.

Mr. McClain squatted down beside the briefcase, shuffled through the papers, saying How sad, a terrible thing, the company was sad, he was personally sad. Here was her pass home, with a special receipt for the box.

And all she had to do was sign here. And here. He stood up and extended a sheaf of papers to her and a fountain pen.

More distinctly than their faces, she always remembered the material their suits were made of. Mr. McClain's was thick and nubby, and the lights cast a shadow beside every nub. The young man with the shoulders had a pale stripe running through the fabric of his suit, and the fat man's suit was plaid, something almost as fine as dress fabric with an open ladder of lines.

The fat man said, "Well, here comes the eastbound train on time for once. Give her the money and let's go home."

Oradell stared at the extended papers. The train pulled in, hissed to a massive stop.

Mr. McClain said, "I think you'll find it's just receipts, statements that you've received what's yours."

The porter got off and watched them from a distance, a silhouette with fuzzy light around his edges. There were dim orange lights in the passenger compartment, and an elderly man looking out.

Mr. McClain touched her shoulder to get her attention and pointed out spaces that needed her signature.

The conductor got down and stood with the porter. They were all looking at Oradell and the box. The conductor took out his watch and said something to the porter. The porter came over and asked the fat man. "How long you holding us for, Boss?"

It was one of Mike's words. These men, who did not even offer her a pop or ask her if she needed to go to the bathroom—they had the power to hold the eastbound train.

"Not long, boy," said the Fat Boss.

McClain wiggled the papers. Oradell clutched her purse with both hands.

"Show her the envelope, Tim," said the Fat Boss.

McClain reached into the briefcase again and came up with a thickly stuffed envelope. He pulled back the flap, ran his thumbnail along the edge of a lot of dollar bills. Then he extended the papers to her again, showing her the money at the same time. She knew she should at least read the papers, but if she tipped her head down to read, tears were going to pour out.

So she said, "How come Mike wasn't in Pennsylvania?"

The Fat Boss answered. "Now how are we supposed to know that, Miss? Maybe he just told you he was going to Pennsylvania. Maybe he had a girlfriend to visit."

"It's a terrible thing," said McClain, "to lose your husband at such a young age."

She said, "Do those papers say what happened to Mike?"

Fat Boss said, "We're giving you cash. Do you want to count the money?" McClain put the papers under his arm and opened the envelope and rifled the dollar bills again.

"Twelve hundred dollars," said Fat Boss.

The one with the big shoulders said, "I wisht somebody paid me that good."

"You'll be home soon, Mrs. Brown," said McClain. "Back with your own people. You'll have a nice funeral."

Oradell thought it was too much money. She knew they were doing this because they wanted her to sign the papers and go away. Something had happened that they wanted ignored. If she signed and took the money and they loaded up the box, it was all over. Whatever happened to Mike would be done and paid for.

She wondered if the eastbound train had a dining car, and did it serve breakfast. She said, "What did he die of?"

At the same moment, the Fat Boss said, "Natural causes," and McClain said, "It was a mine cave-in."

Fat Boss looked irritated. McClain said, "Just sign the papers, Mrs. Brown. Really, it's the best thing you can do. The papers are just like a receipt. They say you received the body, unfortunately crushed by natural causes in a mining accident, and you received compensation."

The train was hissing, and more sleepy faces were looking out the windows to see what was holding them up.

Mike would have made a speech to tell the people to get off the train and give Hell to the Bosses. But Oradell was on her own. The conductor looked at his watch, and the porter looked at the coffin box.

Oradell said, "I don't think a cave-in is exactly goddam natural."

Fat Boss put his hat back on, and so did the one with the shoulders. "You get a ton of coal and rock on your head, you'll be natural dead yourself. Listen, lady, I'm getting tired of this. You're running out of time. Your old man was a Commie. I'm beginning to think you're a Commie too. Your man, he was a goddam red commie, feeding everybody his goddam Commie Baloney. If you're full of goddam red Commie Baloney too, we can just take this money back and leave you here. Is that what you want?"

She wanted to say, Yes! I'm full of whatever Mike was full of! But instead, she was just full of pee and tears. If she signed, she could go to the wash room, go back to sleep, get some bacon and eggs.

McClain said, "Mrs. Brown, we want you satisfied. We don't want you to have any doubts."

She clutched the pocketbook, but knew she was going to open it soon and let them pour the money in. She whispered, "I just don't think a cave-in is natural."

"Well shit," muttered Fat Boss.

"Now, now, she's bereaved," said McClain. "She's mourning the loss of her dear deceased." But then—for all him saying Now Now and keeping his hat off longest—he was maybe the meanest one of all. He said, "Why, we can just jimmy open this box right now and let Mrs. Brown see the way that big chunk of coal stoved in poor Mr. Brown's head."

The one with the big shoulders started to laugh. "Yeah, let's look at how all the blood and guts and brains came squeezing out the corners of his eyes— "

Oradell had a strong stomach, but her body was playing tricks on her tonight, and even with red high heels on, she was the shortest one here.

So when Mr. McClain repeated, "Let's just pry the lid up, honey," Oradell whispered back that was okay, he didn't have to.

"So you're satisfied then?" said McClain.

"Give her the papers, goddam it," said the Fat Boss.

"Here's these papers then."

She signed wherever he pointed: Mrs. Oradell Mike Brown, she wrote. On one line she wrote Oradell Riley Brown, but then she went back to Mrs. Oradell Mike Brown. They didn't care what she wrote. She could have signed Eleanor Roosevelt for all they cared. The one with the big shoulders started to tease her again. "Aw, you better let us open it up, Mrs. Brown. We don't want you to go away thinking there was any foul play. We're sorry for you, honey."

"Just let her finish signing the goddam papers," said Fat Boss.

So she kept signing, and the porter got a rolling cart for the box. Then the Bosses gave her the envelope.

"I want to count it," she said doggedly.

"You just stand here and do that," said Fat Boss. "You just take all night and count it. You can miss the train for all I care. Let's go, boys."

And they turned on their heels, and even McClain didn't say anything else about how sorry he was. They just left, and the conductor said, "All aboard," and the porter said, "You get on board now, Miss."

And she did, without counting the money.

– *10* –

Something heavy was impeding her, a thick thing that stuck to her chest and made it hard to breathe. She thrashed and thumped to get free of it, and finally woke. She was not on the train. It was the ship's prow cutting through water, not the cowcatcher on an old style locomotive. She turned on her light and saw her own room, her bronze and silver jacket where she dropped it on the other bed, her low heeled silver sandals on the floor. Her little refrigerator, the drink she had sipped. Someone was knocking. No, said Oradell. No I won't do it.

"Mrs. Oradell? Can I come in?"

She rose on one elbow. "Stavros? Is that you, Stavros? What time is it?" She didn't say, but wondered, What night is it? Then remembered, trouble in the dining room, men fighting. Panama Canal tomorrow.

He had used his key to come in. He walked toward her slowly, picked up her shoes, picked up her jacket, put it on a hanger.

"What do you want, Stavros?"

Something was going on: he wasn't wearing his steward's coat, just a tight white tee shirt like men used to wear on summer Sunday afternoons before air conditioning. She thought this was probably the first time she'd seen his forearms, which were short and muscular without much hair. "I don't like to wake you, Mrs. Oradell."

Most nights, she would have been glad to see Stavros, even if it was unusual for him to come on his own. "What's up?"

"Jaime got in some trouble at dinner tonight."

"Well I know that. Hard to miss that."

"He don't like Mr. Reese, all the changes, the way Mr. Reese don't respect nobody. Mr. Reese been coming down to quarters, making speeches. I'm gonna fire this one, everyone do this, do that. Jaime lost his temper. It was just a little punch. Mr. Reese, he barely felt nothing. But now he wants to throw Jaime in the brig."

"This boat has a brig?" This was the kind of moment when she wished she still smoked. A cigarette would center things.

"It's just a closet with a lock. It's nothing. Jaime, he should have just go to the brig, spend the night, come out. But not Jaime, he has to run and hide. So now, Mr. Reese, he's going crazy, he's ripping everything apart looking for Jaime." Stavros stood by her bed, holding her metallic jacket on a hanger, waiting.

She said, "That's too damn bad. Jaime's a hothead, but he works hard."

"I say the same thing to Mr. Reese, but he don't like insubordination."

The weight was coming back to Oradell's chest. It was building from the inside out, her heart beating high, slow, and heavy. She wanted to be left alone.

"The boys want to help Jaime."

The thing rising up in her was the impeding thing, the thing that made her sometimes not hear, and it felt like a huge No that you could lay your hands on.

Oradell said, "Let 'em help him. Don't pay any attention to Reese."

"Well, they been hiding him, Mrs. Oradell, but now, Mr. Reese he's having a check of quarters. They're going everywhere."

"Tonight?"

"Like I said, he is damn mad. All the bunks, all the store rooms, everywhere. Making a big search, everyplace down below."

The thing made her limbs heavy and her chest thick. No, she thought, No No No. I never say no when I ought to.

"Stavros," she said, "Leave me alone. I'm an old lady. This kind of excitement is bad for my heart."

For a second, she thought he was going to say more, make a plea. That he was going to ask, Whose side are you on, Oradell? But he only nodded, kept his ordinary expression, hung up her jacket. "Okay, Mrs. Oradell," he said. "No problem. Is there anything you need?"

"Not a thing," said Oradell. "I have everything. I don't need anything."

- *11* -

*A*fter Mike's funeral, Oradell lay around the house watching the food turn green just the way she had when her father died. She picked up where she left off then, before Mike, wearing her father's overalls and waiting for someone to come and save her. The main difference now was that she had the money and she couldn't drink whiskey because she kept throwing up. She went down to the Company store once or twice a day to buy salty snacks and canned lunch meat and pop until Grace Howard sent one of her kids over and told Oradell to come and eat Sunday dinner with them. When she got there, Grace talked to her about having a baby, which Oradell insisted she knew all about already, but was lying. Grace told her she'd better stay with them till the baby came.

She liked staying with the Howards most of the time. Sometimes she got mad at Grace and went back up Shacky Hill for a day or two, but mostly, she was glad to be with the Howards. She was with the Howards when FDR came on the radio to tell them about Pearl Harbor. She was with the Howards through that strange

Christmas, with all the war talk, which she spent in bed because her legs swelled up, and Doctor Wormley told her to get off her feet. The one thing Oradell had always done her whole life was to move around when she felt like it. She flopped in the bed and sulked. Grace said, "For someone who needs to be waited on, Oradell, you are mean as a snake."

Mean as a snake, mad at the world. When someone mentioned Mike Brown, there was a big darkness that came over her forehead and blanked out what was being said. As if she'd never heard of him and didn't intend to. No, she said, No, no, no.

But she didn't cry. She thought about how it wasn't fair that her father froze to death. It wasn't fair she couldn't join the army like Grace's boys. And Bosses shouldn't have made her sign the papers, and Mr. Talkington shouldn't have let her go off alone on the train. And then the darkness closed in around her forehead again and she seemed to be getting bigger and bigger with the baby.

Throughout the rest of her life, Oradell dreamed from time to time of lying in Grace Howard's bed in darkness and then of thrashing and grunting. She would try to keep her body quiet, but it swelled up huge, and she'd have to battle for her breath. Her dream, her actual labor, and all those boring, trammeled days in bed, took place in Grace Howard's front parlor in West Fork. The bed was surrounded by bureaus and end tables and Grace's crocheted antimacassars and little bits of tatting. It faced out on the good side of West Fork: porch swing, boardwalk, view of the baseball fields and river. The day Oradell went into labor, the trees were bristling with irritatingly new leaves.

The brightness wouldn't hold its shape that day. It kept shrinking to a point, and then Oradell started to panic and the suffocation got bigger and kicked and struggled. She wanted out of the room and out of her body. There were waves of pressure and she was afraid to look down. Her body made an enormous groan.

"Relax honey," said Grace, "you're having a baby. So many have done it before you. You're not the first one."

Oradell howled that she didn't want a goddam baby.

"Too late now honey."

Then came Dr. Wormley's scratchy voice from some other part of the room. "Stop that noise, Oradell."

She screamed: "Mrs. Howard! Mrs. Howard! I'm not going to! I'm not going to! I'm not going to have a baby!"

"Oh, yes you are," said Grace.

"Goddam Mike Goddam Brown, Mrs. Howard! Goddam Mike Brown!" For a moment she could think about him: He had talked about the rights of the miners and a better day coming for All Men, but he never said a thing about All Women. "Fuck!" she screamed, "I'm never going to fuck nobody again!"

Dr. Wormley said "Grace, can't you stop that damn girl cussing?"

She had a memory of Dr. Wormley coming over with something then. He was as big as the baby. She was pretty sure he gave her a shot that knocked her out. Looking back, that didn't seem fair either, although at the time she was glad enough.

I didn't know what I wanted, she thought.

Too much of her life she hadn't known what she wanted. The best times were all when she did know: when she saw something before her eyes and went forward. A couple of years later, she wanted to have a different baby, the one that turned out to be Lance. Harry the Ape kicked her in the stomach to get rid of it, but she dodged and fought back. The next thing she wanted was to get away from Harry, and she spent years getting ready to do it. It had been better than being in love to get up before dawn and empty Harry's wallet and start driving East.

But the baby, the first baby, that one just happened, she didn't know what she wanted with it. Everything about it reminded her of what was gone: the baby was small and Mike had been big. It squalled, and he had laughed. She was supposed to take care of it, and Mike took care of her.

Within two weeks of the baby being born, she started going out, leaving the baby with Grace, who yelled at her. But Oradell didn't care. She dressed up and went to the road houses, and met this one and that one, including the traveling man who said he was having beers to build up his courage to drive out of this state with its sidewinder roads. "And never come back!" shouted the man.

"That sounds good to me," said Oradell. "I'll show you how to get out, if you'll take me with you."

And he started smiling and sweating and snuggled her up beside him and said, "What are we waiting for, sweetheart?"

Oradell thought that was all there was to it. She thought that if you could get a man with a car and know how to keep from getting pregnant, you didn't need anyone to save you.

The man took her back to Grace Howard's, and Grace yelled at her for smelling of alcohol. Oradell went straight to her drawer and started filling a cardboard box with clothes. She slipped her envelope of money from the bosses into her brassière just before Grace came in and yelled some more.

She said, "You yell all you want to, Grace, I'm packing up and getting out of here."

"Exactly who with?" said Grace.

"He's right out there in his car," said Oradell, who was hurrying for fear the man wouldn't wait for her.

Grace wanted to know what about the baby, and Oradell said "You can have it, I don't want it. I never wanted that baby, and I don't want it now!"

Grace said some pretty mean things, and Oradell said some pretty mean things, and Grace said the baby was crying, didn't that just pluck at Oradell's heartstrings?

And Oradell said, "I don't even hear it."

In her memory, she still didn't hear it, but she could hear the tone in her own voice, and it hurt her for the poor baby, that its mother would be so mean.

She needn't have worried about her boyfriend running off on her. He was asleep with his forehead on the steering wheel. Oradell shoved him over to the side and drove the car herself, with no license. She drove out of West Virginia by going north to Pittsburgh and then as far west as she could on the gas they had. The man slept all the way, and she kept herself awake with her anger: If you think so much of babies, Grace Howard, you change the goddam diapers.

And Good-bye old Frozen Daddy!

And all the people she knew in West Fork: teachers and kids at the high school, the Talkingtons.

And especially, goddam Mike Brown who said he was going one place and showed up dead somewhere else.

Especially goddam Mike Brown.

And on and on until she ran out of gas coasted into a filling station with a lunch room and just sat there till they opened, and the man woke up, astonished to find Oradell with him and so many miles west already traveled.

- 12 -

What the hell, she thought, sitting up again in the dark, not able to sleep. It was going to be one of those nights that never end. Nowhere near morning yet.

She thought: Why should I help that little cretin Jaime? What did Stavros ever do for me except what he got paid for it? Paid well, too, thank you very much. What did anyone ever do for me? Goddam them all. This was her vacation. Goddam Stavros and Jaime and Mike Brown. She lay back down, covered her face with her blanket and closed her eyes. Her ears seemed to echo with laughter and distant talk in some foreign language that wasn't Spanish, Greek, or Yiddish.

She got up again, went to the toilet, then took a long swallow of gin straight from the bottle.

What's the big deal, she thought. Help the boys out.

She saw Mike, out of reach forever, grinning at her.

She had refused a lot of things because she was mad at Mike. The first time she was aware of it was right after she and Lance moved to New York. I was just this single person, she said, this little small person, struggling to get on as best I could. In New York City for crissake. Why did he keep bothering me? I'm still a little person. Nobody cares what I do. I just try not to get in anyone's way. Leave me alone. I'm not important enough to have regrets. I'm not hurting anyone.

She was living with Lance in a single room occupancy hotel on Broadway in the eighties. Lance was having a growth spurt and seemed to fill up all the space in that overpriced little room, him and his record player. She wasn't sure it had been a good idea to move to the big town, but it was lively and still pretty cheap back in those days. The subways and busses were a dime, and so was a hot dog. She and Lance would go to the park and sit on a bench and eat hot dogs and gape at what all paraded by. She was sure it was a better place for Lance, who even by fifth and sixth grade was a definite oddball. More room for oddballs in a place like this, she would think.

Her first job in New York was at a George's Mart Supermarket. George's was a little chain that went out of business a long time ago and good riddance. When she was working there, Oradell used to say, she might as well have been in the sex trade because of the wandering hands of the manager. Six weeks after she started, she substituted as a waitress at a nice restaurant on the east side, and decided that she was going to leave George's as soon as she could. The restaurant called her to substitute again the next week-end, so she was feeling pretty confident.

On Friday at the grocery store, before her second trial at the restaurant, while she was ringing up a customer with a beard who looked like he had just got up even though it was well after lunch, the manager Napler said Excuse me, he had to get something from the shelf under Oradell's cash register. She remembered clearly that the girl at the other register had a customer too, and the skinny kid who came in after school was shelving canned beans.

Napler squeezed in with Oradell, and right in front of the sleepy-eyed customer with the beard, ran his hand quickly up her leg, under her skirt, all the way to her rear end.

It was one of those moments when everything came together. She had a chance at a better job, it was a hot day when the heat of summer should have been over, and the air conditioning was off, which was typical of George's, the cheap bastards. Napler had made his move in front of four other people, and—maybe mostly—Napler had had liverwurst and onion with mayonnaise for lunch, and she could smell it on his breath.

"Goddam it Napler," she said, and gave him a shove so hard he lost his balance and caught himself by landing on his elbows in the bearded customer's Wonder Bread.

"Hey," said the customer, "you mashed my bread."

Napler backed out of Oradell's cubicle, saying he'd get a new bread, but Oradell was fluid with anger. "Goddam it Napler!" she shouted. "I've had it with you putting your creepy hands on me! I mean it. Did you see that? Did you see what he did?"

"Yeah," said the customer. "I saw it. I saw what he did to my bread too."

"Well I'm not standing for it! I'm leaving! Hey, Maria! Are you standing for it?"

Maria gave one of her shy smiles, and shook her head No. "I'm with you, Oradell," she said, and Oradell felt buoyed up, supported, like her anger wasn't just this free-form cloud, but part of a rising tide, a force to be reckoned with.

"This guy's hands are all over every girl who ever worked here," said Oradell to the customer. Napler reappeared with a fresh Wonder Bread.

The man said he sure wouldn't stand for it.

Oradell yelled at Maria, "Are you going to stay in here?"

Maria shook her head.

"Well then let's walk out of here!"

Everyone was sweating, and underlying Napler's liverwurst breath was some bad smell emanating from the meat cooler. To Oradell's surprise, the kid unpacking beans stood up and shouted, "Me too!"

"All right then!" said Oradell. "We're walking out!" said Oradell. "Come on you all! We're going on goddam strike!"

And they walked out: Oradell and Maria and the bearded customer and the kid with the beans in his hands. Napler followed them. Maria's customer hung back, and it turned out later that she had filled her pocketbook with a few odd items off the shelves. Napler didn't notice because he was running after them waving the unmashed Wonder Bread in the air, hopping up and down as if he were part of the walk-out too.

"You girls get back in here! I'm calling Mr. George!"

"You call Mr. George!" yelled Oradell. "I have a thing or two to say about old Mr. George and his broken air conditioning and his rotten meat!" Some people were stopping to watch, so Oradell shouted, "The manager feels up employees! Yeah, that guy right there! Don't shop at George's!"

It was hot outside too, but the late summer sun falling on the back of their necks was better than the stale shop air. Oradell started feeling really good. She yelled at a passing cab with a open window, "Napler pinches the employees!"

The cab driver honked his horn.

The customer who had stayed inside to pick up a few things finally came out and looked right and left and hurried away. The man with the beard, though, Oradell's customer, turned out to be some kind of left-wing pinko. He stayed around and helped them make up slogans: "No fair, no work! George's exploits its employees!"

It was great. Oradell remembered it as one of her happiest moments in New York. It was how they were laughing and chanting together, Oradell and Maria, the kid and the pinko, people passing by, everyone yelling about George's.

Meanwhile, Napler had called the boss, and Mr. George—who was known to be pretty quick with his hands himself—arrived from his other store, and some cops showed up about the same time, and Mr. George smoothed it all over, yelled at Napler and told him he was on in-store suspension, and told the employees they could all have free steaks for dinner. Oradell cooked hers that night and she and Lance both got stomach aches, so she always suspected the bad smell from the cooler had been the meat. That would be just like George too. If you can't screw the employees one way, screw them another.

Finally, everything quieted down and they went back to work, and a few people who had been standing around came in and bought soda to show their support for the successful outcome. Mr. George gave everyone free match books with his name on them and hand-shakes and big smiles. He stayed around in his tight shiny suit, and finally, when there were no customers, he whispered to Oradell through a big smile that he hoped she wasn't going to turn out to be a trouble maker.

And Oradell said, with an equally big smile, slick as butter, "No sir, Mr. George, I never meant to make trouble, but I'm a mother and I want to be treated with respect."

For the next couple of days Mr. George dropped in a lot and Napler stayed mostly in the stock room. Meanwhile, the fancy restaurant kept calling Oradell. Things were going her way.

Oradell said No to Mike Brown a week later, after her shift ended and she had started walking home. Halfway up the block a young man blocked her way. She lifted her chin and squared her pocketbook, ready to brush him off, but he said "Hi Oradell!" and pushed his cap back into his curly dark hair.

And Oradell saw Mike Brown standing in front of her on the streets of New York City.

Of course it wasn't Mike, and she knew it pretty quickly, one thing about Oradell was that she always had her feet on the ground. But he was just the size of Mike, bow legged like Mike. Had Mike's hair and smile. And knew her name. Her mouth was dry, and she couldn't get out the words at first, not even a simple How do you know my name?

But the teeth in his big grin were straighter than Mike's, and he was at least ten years younger than Mike would be if he were alive.

In spite of having her feet on the ground, she wanted to hear him say he was not Mike, and also that he was not her baby, and he couldn't have been her baby, her baby was a girl. "Who are you? How do you know my name?"

He said his name was Joe and he wanted to buy her a beer and talk to her a little while.

"No," she said. "I have to get home to my kid. What do you want? Why do you know my name?"

"Please," he said. "How about a coffee? It's business, I need to talk some business to you. Five minutes?"

"No," she said, but she was curious.

His eyes crinkled at the corners: it was after all a different face from Mike's, a little fuller, a different nose. But it could have been Mike's son. "I just need ten minutes," said Joe.

"I thought it was five."

"I'm from the Union," he said.

She wondered if he was Mike's son.

She went around the corner with him to a little newsstand with a counter. He had a longish body compared to his short legs. He rolled when he walked, and the curls on his forehead bounced, he kept flashing her his smile, to keep her coming along, so she wouldn't run away. This was around 1960 or 62, and she was wearing ballet flats that hurt her feet after standing all day in the grocery store, but everything stopped hurting when she walked with him. She was already saying No in her mind. Goddam Mike Brown, she thought, goddam.

Joe insisted on ordering pie with the coffee, and he dug in, elbows on the counter.

"Now where did you get my name?" she said. "I don't give out my name to strangers."

The Union had heard about her little demonstration, and they asked around, talked to the kid who worked afternoons, found out Oradell was the one who started it.

"I didn't do it for any union," said Oradell. "I did it because Napler pinched my butt."

Joe was like Mike too in the way he listened. It wasn't so much that he was paying attention to what you said as that he paid attention to *you*—he liked you, whatever you said. He was also like Mike because he had his own agenda. He liked you, and he needed to get you on his side.

But Oradell didn't listen to him either. He had a bumpier nose than Mike, and he was stockier. But that could be his mother's people, she thought.

The union was trying to organize some of the small places, he told her, especially the little chains like George's, and George had an especially bad reputation.

"You're telling me," said Oradell. She kept trying to do the math: How old had Mike been when she last saw him? How old was this guy? The numbers, the dates kept slipping and sliding around her. She never knew exactly how old Mike was anyhow. He had been at least thirty, maybe thirty five. He had been twice her age, and Grace Howard never trusted him, and who was to say he hadn't had a wife or a girl friend in New York City with little Joe toddling around?

What the union needed was for people to sign the cards. To get a fair shake from cheap bastard Mr. George.

In the end, had Mike really been any different from Napler, except that he smelled better?

"So what do you think?" said Joe.

"What do I think about what?"

"Can you help us out? Get some cards signed?"

"Not interested," she said.

He didn't look fazed. "Let me tell you what the union can do for you."

"I know that story," she said, but of course Joe told it to her anyhow. It was Mike's story, a little different, a little less about all the people in the whole world rising up together, but it was still about people standing shoulder to shoulder and doing things together that nobody could do alone. Being enclosed in that rich smell of togetherness. It was a good story, and part of her wanted to shout, Yes, I'll do it for Mike! For all of us.

But the angry No was bigger. It took hold in her chest. It had come over her when Baby was born. I am not this. This is not me.

Oradell wondered if Joe's mother had been Mike's real wife, or maybe Mike had a dozen wives in a dozen cities, and children like puppies resembling him around the country, wherever Working Men were out on strike.

Oradell started smiling back at Joe, showing him he wasn't the only one who could charm people. She said No, probably not, maybe, she didn't know, she had a kid, she needed the job, she was looking out for number one, she had never been a joiner.

And Joe's face got pink, and he pushed back his cap and curls in his excitement, working to convince her. And all the time it was Oradell who had him on the line, leaning forward, being receptive and all the time cold and angry in her mind Goddam you Mike Brown. Not this time. And to Joe: who was your father? What bitch is your mother? Did you ever meet Mike Brown?

"You don't know what you're talking about," she told him at one point, meaning how Mike had left her, had gotten himself killed and left her not only pregnant, but so angry that she was choked with No.

And she also wanted to tell him that Mike Brown was the best thing that ever happened to her—and how she had never forgiven him.

Joe's forehead wrinkled, he lowered his face with determination. "Hey it's never easy, I'm not saying there's no risk involved. I'm just saying it's worth it."

When it was over, she took the slip of notebook paper with Joe's phone number, took a little stack of union cards and a brochure, and gave him a phone number too, but not her real one. Then she stood on the street and waved good-bye to Joe, bow-legged, bouncy, off to organize some more working people.

She went back into George's and got her blue cardigan sweater out of the bathroom and shoved it in her purse. She said good-bye again to Maria and never went back.

Walked ten blocks, tore up the phone number and union cards.

Now it's over, Mike Brown, she had said. Now you'll leave me alone.

Only of course he didn't. Being angry at him all over again didn't keep him out of her mind. He came in dreams and shook his head sadly. Leave me the fuck alone, Mike, she would say. Didn't you see what I did to you? I threw away your union! You fathered babies in New York City and you knocked me up and you lied to me and now you're trying to say I'm the one who did wrong?

But of course Oradell was the one accusing. She had no idea if he'd fathered other babies. And even if he had, irrespective of whether Mike lied to her or whether she had been paranoid about him having families elsewhere or how bad off she'd been when he died, he was still right about the working man, and she was wrong to refuse.

You have to help people in trouble, and people have to stand together for what's fair. So she turned on her light one more time and called Stavros.

- 13 -

When Stavros came in, he had his steward's coat back on.

"I changed my mind," she said. "I want to help. Do you still need me to hide Jaime?"

"It's okay, Mrs. Oradell," said Stavros. "It's okay—we got him hid— "

"Not good enough or you wouldn't have asked me in the first place."

"I didn't ask."

"Yes you did. You figure Reese won't bother passengers, so this is the best place for him. Bring him here for tonight—just for tonight only—while Reese is doing the check."

She thought Stavros was going to turn her down. Maybe the bed check was already over. Stavros opened his mouth, closed it, nodded. "Maybe just for tonight, Mrs. Oradell," he said. "That would be fine."

They need me for this, Oradell thought, a little amazed at how close she had come to not helping. "Hell, yes, I'll help old Jaime," she said. "What could they do to me anyhow? I'm a rich bitch passenger."

She sat on her bed. She was just thinking of having a drink or going to the toilet again when the lock turned and Stavros more or less pushed Jaime into her room, still wearing his rumpled waiter's jacket.

"Jaime, man," she said, "why did you do what you did?"

Jaime's eyes were bloodshot and sullen. "Because Reese is a *maricón*."

Stavros said, "Just till they finish the inspection, Mrs. Oradell, then I'll get him out of here."

"I'm in for this one night, Stavros, all night if you want, but just don't think I'm going to hide him for the rest of the cruise."

"We'll go through the Canal tomorrow, Mrs. Oradell, and then we'll stop in Cristobal. We'll sneak him off there. We got it all planned."

Jaime's heavy eyebrows pulled together. "I don't like fokkin Panama. I'm not getting off in goddam fokkin hell hole Cristobal Panama."

Oradell said, "Well, it don't look to me like you got a lot of choice, Jaime. I don't know what Mr. Reese has in mind, but if I were you, I'd get out while the getting is good."

Jaime said, "I got a cousin in Colombia. I want to get off at Cartagena."

Oradell said, "You better get out in Panama."

Jaime shook his head doggedly. "I don't like fokkin Panama."

"Goddam, Jaime, you are too dumb to move the shit house."

Stavros said, "Jaime, don't give Mrs. Oradell a hard time. Mrs. Oradell, you go back to sleep, I'll turn off the light, you never know he's here. But I got to go back, they want to know where I am."

"Sure, go along. Leave the light on. Jaime and me, we'll be fine."

"Just one hour," said Stavros. "I give you everything free for this, Mrs. Oradell, the rest of the trip, whatever you want."

"Don't be a dope, Stavros. Keep it business. I'm just doing this for the fun of it. This is part of the recreation."

When Stavros was gone, Jaime stood in the middle of her room, his hands tightly fisted, his head lowered.

She said, "Jaime, you look like hell. But, what the hell, right? They haven't caught you yet. You need a drink." She levered her body over so that she could reach the wine goblets in the night stand.

He accepted the drink, and she pointed at the other bed. He sat, knocked back the drink in one swallow, then stared stolidly at the wall. His slightly jowly face with the features all close together reminded her of some kind of dog she couldn't think of the name of.

She said, "You're not very good company, Jaime."

"I work hard!" he said. "I work goddam fokkin hard, Mrs. Oradell!"

"You don't have to tell me waiting tables is hard work. I spent more years waiting tables than you are old."

"I got a family! How come this fokkin shithead losing me my job?"

"Because you punched him, Jaime. You can't go around punching people."

"He went after me already before that. He don't like me. He came on this cruise looking for people to fire. Now he says he going to get me in jail, make sure I never work on a ship again. I didn't do nothing!"

"You hit him in the nose."

"I missed! I wish I hit him in the nose. I been thinking all night what I'd like to do to his fokkin summabitch nose."

"Well, I'd talk to Reese for you, but he doesn't like me very much either. You're right, though, he is looking for folks to fire." If Mike had lived, she thought. If, somehow, in some other world, it was her and Mike on this cruise, two senior citizens who had saved up, and this was, say, their first real vacation. Or maybe it was a present from their kids. She wouldn't have been carrying around this stupid anger if Mike had lived. If Mike was here, he would explain it all, make everything fall into place.

She said, "Look here, Jaime. As far as I can see, that Mr. Reese, the story with him is, he's for the Bosses. That's all. What the bosses do is, they make money. All over the world. They run things, they make the money. They don't care if Reese throws his weight around and fires somebody with a family. They don't even know about it. He can do what he wants to, as long as he saves them some money. It's not personal."

"*He*'s personal. He's goddam fokkin summabitch personal."

"You better get off in Panama, Jaime. In Panama, at least they speak Spanish. You should be okay."

"I want to go home to P.R.," he said.

"Oh come on. That's five days away. There's no way the boys can hide you that long."

"Okay, Cartagena. But not Cristobal. Cristobal's a fokkin stink hole."

"Whatever you say, Jaime, honey, but the longer you stay on board, the more chance of him catching you. He seems like a pretty determined son-of-a-bitch."

"He's a goddam fokkin personal summabitch."

"Yeah, right. You got it." She made Jaime take another drink, then turned the lights off. She hadn't had much of her drink. She felt sober and cheerful. After a while, she said into the darkness, "Jaime, are your wife and kids in San Juan?"

He grumbled softly, and for a second she thought he was already asleep, but the grumble turned into sentences: "I got beautiful children, I got a house. Up in the mountains. You go up the road up from Arecibo, far far up. You drive and drive. My wife, she wants to go live in the city, I say you stay in the mountains. She say she can get a job, I say you keep the kids safe up in the mountains. Too much bad in the cities. Too dangerous."

"That's right," said Oradell. "Sometimes I wish I'd taken Lance to the mountains."

"My wife says, there's nothing in the mountains but oranges. I say that's right, there's oranges on the trees! You can reach out of the car, you can stop where you're walking, wherever you go, just reach out and pick oranges."

"We have nice trees back home in West Virginia, but no oranges."

Then Jaime's voice sank down again, and he grumbled some more, but in Spanish now. Oradell kept saying, "That's right, you got that right all right," for a while, then she closed her eyes. To Jaime, home was oranges. She hadn't been home in thirty years. She made one trip only, after the baby was born. How can there be thirty years of anything in one life?

She needed to pee. "That's why you need a husband to get old with," she said, but Jaime had gone silent. "You need someone you can talk to about your bowels. Not that I'm too prissy to tell anyone if I feel like it, but it's a bore, your bowels and your piss, and your breathing. You have a wife or a husband, you trade off. He tells you his, you tell him yours."

She closed her eyes, trying to hold her story a little longer, imagining it was Mike Brown in the other bed, that he had come back to her, they had got old together.

- 14 -

*O*radell woke with a sense of unfinished business. It wasn't about Jaime. He was gone, and she was glad. Good, that's over, she thought. I did my part. It's daylight, it's Panama Canal Day. She ate the roll and juice Stavros had left her. She had to do something. She opened the shades, and the brilliance of light that fell into her room made her whistle; she rarely opened her shades so early. She rarely got up so early.

It was Lance. She wanted to go to the bridge during radiophone hours and call Lance.

She put on her cork wedgie sandals decorated with plastic oranges and plums, then some bracelets made of hand-painted bananas and grapes strung on elastic. She picked a purple gauze caftan and the straw hat with the purple ties. The hat and caftan were new, bought in Acapulco the day before the cruise started. She had a woman there who owned a boutique and brought arm loads of stuff to her hotel room for her to look at. You didn't even have to go shopping if you didn't want to, if you were rich enough.

The caftan had a lining, but her nipples still showed. What the hell, she thought. If you got it, flaunt it.

She gave herself another good once over in the mirror and said, "It's Chiquita Prune Juice." She liked purple and red and bangles and rings, but necklaces still made her nervous.

Out on deck there was an amazing high sky, and the ocean was silver and almost flat. No land in sight, but spread out in all directions were dozens of silent ships waiting their turn to go through the Canal. Oil tankers mostly, one private yacht. Waiting like planes stacked for landing, but ranged out, not up. For so many days, the *Golden Argonaut* had been totally alone on the Pacific, and now there was a crowd. After the Canal came the ports: Cristobal, Cartagena, Caracas, Aruba, San Juan. Shopping, beaches, sight-seeing.

"It's damn flat out there," she said to a man standing a little way down the rail from her. "Not a wave on the sea or a cloud in the sky." He smiled at her agreeably. He was thick in the middle and wearing white loafers. A round faced woman in a flowery print sundress joined him. They looked like nice people. She hadn't noticed them before. They must be in the other dinner seating. There were probably a lot of people on board that she hadn't noticed. That's what happened when you slept late every day.

There were a lot of other people on deck too. People got excited about the Canal. They drank champagne with lunch and had sex while the ship was in the locks. The recreation staff handed out quizzes. How long is the Canal? When was the first transit? How long between the first surveying and the beginning of construction?

And, thought Oradell, how many boys died building it? The recreation staff would never put that on their quizzes.

She started up the stairs by the pool. There was a seaman scraping some paint off the railing. His back was to her, his whites taut over his rear end. He was stretching his neck to see something, a girl lounging by the pool. It was Tracy Weston in a two piece bathing suit. White.

Oradell said, "Looks good enough to eat, don't she, honey buns?"

When he saw that Oradell was smiling, he smiled too and shrugged.

"You too, honey," she said. "You're not bad yourself." She winked, and he nodded.

She waved at Tracy, but Tracy was behind sunglasses and either had her eyes closed, or, more likely, was still mad because Oradell had snarled last night and refused to let her walk her to her room. Oradell sat on the lounge next to Tracy and shoved a finger in her ribs.

"What!" Tracy sat up. "Oh, it's you."

"Sorry I was such a bitch last night."

Tracy pulled up the back of her chair and looked over her sunglasses at Oradell. She was only pouting a little.

Oradell said, "There was something about that whole deal with Jaime that got me in a rotten mood."

Tracy said, "I heard the waiters are hiding him."

"Could be."

"I offered to help," said Tracy.

"Don't bother," said Oradell. "He'll do fine without any help from you."

"I assumed you'd be like, Solidarity With the Poor Waiters."

"Honey, I clawed and scratched my way to where I am thanks to nobody-goddam-it-else-except-my-own-self.

Take your whining begging charities and shove them where the sun don't shine."

Tracy looked skeptical. "You told me you always carry cash for beggars. You told me you got rich just because Morris Greengold happened to sit at your table."

"So? Your point?"

"You're contradicting yourself! I mean, how can you be proud of where you are if you got there just by being lucky—"

Oradell thought maybe she should have saved making up with Tracy till later, to make sure she got her phone call in. "Look here, sister, stop trying to catch me up. I never had time in my life to make sure my thoughts matched up like color-coordinated tops and pants."

"I just think it's interesting that you say you made yourself and nobody ever helped you, but you also say it's nothing but luck you aren't still a waitress with bad legs— "

"Aching legs," said Oradell. "I never said *bad* legs. I always had very good legs."

"—and you also say we should help the downtrodden. I'm not saying I disagree, just that it's a contradiction." Tracy swung her gorgeous young legs around so that she and Oradell were knee to knee and face to face. Tracy's were longer than Oradell's had ever been, and tanner, of course.

"I never had the luxury of sitting around being philosophical like you kids today."

Tracy said, "You're lumping me with all the other kids in my generation again. Nobody in my generation philosophizes! I wish I knew somebody who philosophizes! The kids in my school cut class and go to the beach and smoke marijuana."

"Same difference," said Oradell.

"No, it's not! And I hate those kids and that whole California scene. Philosophy is something smart people do—"

"I wouldn't know," said Oradell.

"You're smart!"

"Well, I guess that's another goddam contradiction then, isn't it? You can be smart and not have time to think and then you can be smart and have time and still not think."

Tracy rolled her eyes and sucked her teeth, and Oradell felt pleased with herself. That was pretty good, she thought, that you could be smart and not have time to think and smart and have time and still not think. Of course, she hadn't won any wars with Tracy though, probably not even a battle. Tracy would keep on until she got what she wanted.

"I'm going," said Oradell. "I want to call up my boy Lance."

Tracy's face changed. "Not yet, I have to tell you something!"

Oh Lord, thought Oradell, the Love Stuff.

"I was talking to Nikko today. This morning."

"Yes?"

"And he is, you know, he's had a lot of things happen in his life. He reminds me of you that way, I mean he's closer to my age, but he's been through a lot. He's very interesting."

"Good, I'm glad you like each other."

"Oh, like," said Tracy, impatiently. "Like!"

"Don't knock it, honey."

"What I wanted to tell you was, what I said to you the other day, it was a lie."

Oradell had no idea what she was talking about.

"When I said I would never have sex except in a great passion? Well, it isn't true. I think there are other reasons to have sex. And I did have sex. Just one time, and it wasn't about passion or love. It was at a party last summer at this kid's house. He's like really rich, and his parents are always traveling, and the staff is supposed to watch him, but they just stay in their wing of the house and let him party. Then they come out and clean up so they don't get in trouble. Anyhow, this guy, not the one whose house it was at, another one, stood up on the bar around eleven o'clock and made, like, an announcement that he was disposing of anyone's virginity who wanted to have it done. He'd be in the cabana beside the pool. Everyone laughed at him, but this girl and I, we drank a lot of vodka and went up to the cabana, and there he was, and we had him do it."

Oradell felt a little puff of sadness, but she said, "It takes a real young fella to have that kind of stamina."

"What do you think? Tell me your honest opinion."

"About having sex like that? I don't know. Sex is a funny thing. Some of the best sex I ever had was with the worst men. Lance's father, for example. That man was the biggest mistake of my life, I mean, he robbed me and he used me, and he hit me. But, honey, when we weren't beating on each other with blunt instruments, we made music. Great sex. I don't suppose your first time was any worse than a lot of people's first time. Nobody made you do it, and you had a friend with you."

"She's not my friend anymore. Not because of that, but she's just totally untrustworthy. But I wanted you to know, I've been celibate ever since. Except for a blow job. Well, two blow jobs. That's just something to do because it's easier than making a big deal about it. But no real sex." Primly, with her legs so smooth and brown, her elbows on her knees, her chin in her hands. "But now I want to have an affair with Nikko."

Oradell thought she should have stayed out of this thing with Tracy and Nikko. She wanted to tell all the young people, Yes, yes, sex is terrific, nothing quite like it, but it isn't a big deal. You're going to be doing it for the next fifty or sixty years. You'll do it in as many moods as you eat dinner. So relax.

"I've decided that I'm going to have an affair with Nikko. When we talked this morning—"

"Spare me the details, Tracy. I wish you well, you should enjoy life, and be sure you don't get pregnant, but, please, don't give me the details. Okay? I've got my own life."

"Okay," Tracy smiled. When she smiled, her face was rounder, with dimples.

Oradell grunted her way to her feet. "You do know about birth control, don't you?"

"My mom got me fitted with a diaphragm ages ago. She's like this schizophrenic, you know? She does something like that and then acts like it never happened."

"That's good," said Oradell. "Nikko's a doll baby, but I don't know that he's exactly the responsible type."

"I don't want to marry him, I just want, I just want—"

"Yeah, I know. You want to have a good ride through life. Feel that old motorcycle engine between your legs."

Tracy giggled. "I'll walk you up."

It was the blood, Oradell thought, all that blood everyone had pounding through them and how much they all wanted to live. "I'm feeling fine today. You stay here and take the sun for me. I don't go out in the sun anymore."

Tracy said, "I wish you'd been my mother!"

And Oradell thought, surprising herself: And I wish I'd kept mine and Mike's little girl.

She hadn't been to the bridge of the *Golden Argonaut* in two years or maybe three. Usually, she called Lance from the Acapulco Princess before she left and then from the Caribe Hilton when she got to San Juan. She was out of breath by the time she got to the bridge, so she sat down for a while on the banquette. There were windows to the sea on three sides and on the other a window to the navigator's chart room. She could see some of the ships's officers in there, moving at a relaxed pace. That's always good, she thought, you like to see calm in there. One thing you never want to see is excited airline pilots and ship's navigators.

She sat a long time, lulled by the nice clean men in white uniforms working. After a while, the First Mate came out and spoke to her. He offered to set her up with a phone, and she said, "When I was a kid in West Virginia, I didn't even have a phone and here I am calling New York City from the Panama Canal."

It was only when she had the phone in her hand that she realized she wasn't sure why she was calling Lance. He hadn't been in when she called from Acapulco, so she wanted to hear his voice, and she always had things to remind him of. She had been reminding him of things all his life: Lance, honey, do you have money in your wallet? Lance, did you take your pill? Lance, you don't want to eat that whole pint of chocolate ripple do you?

But this was about the Baby. She had never told Lance about the baby. She didn't want him to hear first about the baby when some damn lawyer read him the will. Not that she was about to die. And not that Lance wasn't going to get his share. He was going to be a very comfortably-off boy. Or middle-aged man. But she didn't want him to hear from a lawyer that she was also leaving money to the baby.

Lance's voice was fuzzy and muffled.

"Did I wake you, honey?" she said.

"Hi Mom." She could hear him stirring around. He would be sitting up, looking at the clock. "You're not back, are you?" he said.

"No, we're waiting our turn to go through the Panama Canal. Sorry I woke you."

"Oh, it's time to get up. You're at the Canal?"

"Yep. Waiting our turn. We're about to say bye-bye to the flying fish. They only live on the Pacific side, you know."

She could hear the yawn in his voice. "So how's the cruise?" He had always had the sweetest temper. He had a deliberateness, a slowness. He had been bigger than Oradell from the time he was twelve. She was so glad to hear his voice. She tended to forget people when she wasn't with them, even Lance. His bigness, his sweetness. "The cruise is fine, honey. How's the weather up there?"

"Cold and dry. No snow. Could be a lot worse."

"So what are you doing?"

"I'm working on a deal, Mom. Some people I know are trying to get up a show off-Broadway and I may help produce it—"

"With what?"

141

"Now don't start, mom. This is a low budget deal. It's not like I was spending the principal— "

"Damn straight you're not."

"You'll love this show. It's not a revue, it's an actual drama, it will make you cry."

"I don't want to cry."

"Well, it will make you laugh then. It's got everything. Wait and see. You'll like it. You sound good, Mom."

She laughed. "You make me feel good, baby."

"Have you got a new boyfriend?"

"No, have you got a new boyfriend?"

"I'm bad at relationships, Mom, you know that."

"I was a bad role model. I should have found you a father. Do you remember how mad you were when you found out Mike Brown wasn't your daddy?"

"He was all you talked about. No wonder I thought he was my father."

Oradell had let him think it for a while, but finally had a moment of honesty and told him the truth. Lance had been down at the mouth for a couple of days. "I thought I got the *good* daddy," he had said.

And Oradell had said, "Oh honey, your daddy had some good things about him too."

So of course Lance wanted to know what the good things were.

And Oradell thought: Well, let's see, he could drink more than any man I ever knew and still stand up. He was real slick at stealing money out of a lady's purse. But she said, "He was a charming fellow. He was big and handsome like you're going to be."

Lance had waited for more.

"And he could sing. Your own daddy could sing as good as Frank Sinatra. He would have been a big star if he had ever had any luck."

Lance said, "Are you okay Mom? The last time you called me from a ship you were in sick bay."

"I never."

"The year you broke your ankle."

"Oh that."

"I wish you wouldn't be too hard-headed to see a doctor," he said. "I worry about you."

"Damn doctors," said Oradell. "Don't talk to me about doctors."

"Oh Mom."

She almost laughed when he said Oh Mom. He had said it with exactly the same tone of voice from the time he could talk. "It's just that I've been thinking. I think about things out here on the ocean. I wanted to tell you something about my will—"

"*Are* you feeling okay, Mom?"

"I'm fine! Shut up, Lance. The time to talk about these things is when you're fine, everyone knows that. I want to be the one to tell you how I made an adjustment in my will, and I don't want you to be surprised when you hear about it. I want to be the one to tell you, now. While I'm still on top of the world. Okay?"

There was a silence. He would be wearing his velours robe. The apartment was cool and shadowed in the morning because it faced west. Radiators fizzled in the winter. They could have bought a big jazzy modern place, but they liked the old co-op on Riverside Drive. It had a view and lots of big rooms, a fine, well-kept building: two rooms for her, her own bathroom, most of the rooms for Lance, a maid's room for guests. They had watched the Macy's Fourth of July fireworks on the Hudson River from their living room window. It made her happy to know the apartment was there, with Lance in it. She'd had the accountant draw up a special trust fund just to pay for the maintenance on the apartment so Lance could always live there.

Lance said, "So Mom, what's up? Are you threatening to leave me out of the will like Morris and his kids?"

"Just listen, okay? Mr. Big Mouth? The safe deposit box. You know you have to go straight down there and get everything out first thing if you ever hear something happened to me—"

"Mom, you've told me twenty times. I know all about that."

"Do you know where the key is?"

"Yes, Mom. The key is in your small bureau drawer with your earrings."

"Well, there's something else, I don't want you to be surprised. I'm leaving a little bit of money to someone you didn't know about— "

"You *do* have a new boyfriend!"

"No, I don't. It's for the baby. You don't know about the baby. I'm leaving some money to the baby. I wanted to tell you about the baby."

"What baby?"

"Mine and Mike Brown's. Your big sister. She's probably a grandma by now, but I always think of her as the Baby. I ran out on her. I still feel bad about it. I was mad at Mike Brown for dying, so I ran out on her."

Lance was quiet for a minute. "Oh," he said. "I know who you mean. I saw her picture once."

"No you didn't. I never told you a word about her."

"You didn't show me, that lady showed me. Your aunt or whoever she was, the time when I was real small and we went to visit whoever she was in West Virginia. The one who always sent Christmas cards."

"Grace Howard."

"Yeah."

"You were only five years old!"

"I don't know how old I was, but you went out of the room, and she showed me a picture. She had a picture of a girl in her pocket book. I always remember that, because she said, 'That's your sister, little boy, what do you think of that?' And I said, 'I don't have a sister,' and she said, 'Oh yes you do, and this is her picture.'"

"Goddam Grace Howard," said Oradell. "I thought I was keeping this big secret from you. I always felt so bad because I never got in touch with the Baby. Her address is in the drawer with the safe deposit key."

"You've had her address and never got in touch?"

"I have different addresses. I used to have an address for the family she lived with—I don't even know if there was an official adoption. Things were more informal back then. But according to Grace they treated her the same as if she was theirs, and that's what counts. When Morris died, and I had some disposable income, I got a detective to find her. That's the most recent address I have. I never called her, but I put her in the will."

"You should have called her, Mom, if you wanted to do something for her."

"I'm not asking for your opinion. I'm a coward, and it's too late anyhow. I'm too old to call her up, she's an old lady herself."

"Okay, mom," said Lance, who didn't like commotion. "I'm glad you're putting her in the will. You're right to do it. So don't feel bad." Then he changed the subject, told her that Myrna and Cantinflas the chihuahuas had got fleas and he had no idea how. About a leak in the closet from the upstairs apartment and no one even knew that any pipes ran through there.

"Would you rather have had an apartment in one of those new high-rises?" she asked.

"Never!" he said. "Are you kidding? Do those places have plaster sunbursts on the ceiling? You know I love this place, Mom!" They were silent then, and she was about to say good-bye, but he asked, "Mom, what if I called her? How would you feel about that?"

"I'm the one who should do it."

"If I did it, it might be easier for everyone."

"Well," said Oradell, "I certainly wouldn't stop you. The envelope about her is in my bureau, under some old silk panties with no elastic. It just says 'Baby'."

He always cheered her up. She loved him for making her feel good, or maybe it was the other way around, that loving him was what made her feel good.

Damn philosophical this morning, aren't we, she thought, waving to the officers as she went out. She took her time going down, and ran into the Old Man himself, lumbering up to the bridge.

"Beautiful, beautiful, happy happy!" he said, and kissed her fingers. She thought of saying something to him about Jaime, but she was full of her own unfinished life, to Hell with Jaime. She liked having her fingers kissed.

- 15 -

*T*he last time Oradell visited West Fork was when Lance was five, the time he saw the picture of the Baby. They had been driving across the United States, escaping Harry, on the way to Allentown, Pennsylvania, where Oradell stayed a couple of years before going on to New York. It was still early as they drove toward Pittsburgh, and she suddenly had a picture in her mind of West Fork, as if she were standing again in front of the Talkingtons' house. She turned the Ford south.

After driving a while, she asked Lance if he would like to try one of the best hot dogs anyone ever ate, and Lance, who was always serious when it came to food, wanted more details about the hot dogs, and then said yes, he'd like that very much. He was a good traveler, not restless, always staring out the window hugging his stuffed animal, which was either a rabbit or a long-eared dog.

She said, "Do you know what, Lance, honey, the place with the hot dogs is where Mommy lived when she was a little girl your age."

"At the hot dog store?"

"No! But in the same town!"

"Loopy wants to see," he said. That was Lance's way of being polite. Loopy was the stuffed animal, and whenever Lance was unsure about something, he would attribute a feeling to Loopy.

After a while, Lance said, "Loopy's getting hungry."

"Yeah, he can have some hot dogs with us. It's just a little bitty hot dog stand, don't look like much, but oh they make the best hot dogs. It's where the street car used to stop."

"I'll look forward to that," said Lance, smiling out the window.

She probably should have worried back then that Lance didn't want to be outside running around with the other little boys, but what did she know? She was still an ignorant kid herself. She enjoyed having Lance around, and always figured that whatever problems Lance had as an adult were Harry the Asshole's fault. Anyhow, Lance had turned out just fine: different from most, and too kind hearted to make it big in show business, but a pleasure to be around.

That last trip to West Fork seemed to take forever. Across the river at Point Marion, down through Morgantown with the University rising up on all those hills, through Fairmont, dominated back then by Hartley's Department Store. Church chimes playing hymns. It was too early in the spring for leaves, so everything seemed sunny and bare. It was this barren, yellow, early spring look that West Fork had when she dreamed of it.

The highway narrowed between the river and the hillside just before West Fork, and Oradell's heart started to speed up. There were the big West Side houses. She wondered whatever happened to Sarah Ellen, maybe a teacher now, but more likely married.

The first shock was that the street car tracks were gone, and the street car station too. She glanced over at Lance and decided she wouldn't tell him right away that there was no hot dog stand. There was a filling station open, though, so she pulled in and bought gas.

Oradell got out of the car, shook her skirt and stretched. The filling station boy had unfashionably long hair. Otherwise cute enough, and Oradell herself was still pretty hot in those days, and she always dressed up when she traveled. She had thin hips and good legs, and was not above stretching her back and waggling her butt when she was around men. "I grew up in this town," she said. "I been gone a long while now. But I grew up over on Mud Street or as some called it Shacky Hill. Do they still call it Shacky Hill?" He shrugged like he might know or he might not. "Yeah," said Oradell. "That was a long time ago."

The boy said, "Was it as dead around here then as it is now?"

"To tell you the truth, it seemed pretty lively to me. Of course, I guess you have more going on a week-day, don't you?"

"No," he said. He didn't offer to wash her wind-shield. And her always boasting how people back home were so good to help you out.

Harry Asshole used to say, Then go to goddam back home, hillbilly whore.

No-good sonofabitch. Good-bye, Farewell, It's been Hell to know you.

She said, "Are the mines still working?"

"Off and on."

"So you boys can still go down there and make a lot of money?"

"Not me. You won't catch me down in the mines. I'm going to be a singer."

"Like Frank Sinatra?"

"Like Tex Ritter."

"Good old Tex," she said. "He's got the nicest voice." The boy seemed to soften up or wake up. He washed the windshield after all. "Why, thanks, honey," she said. "When I left West Virginia, I couldn't get out fast enough, but you know, wherever I go, I always talk about how nice folks are back home."

She gave him a dime when she paid, because he did the windshield, but also because she always tipped people. Her dad used to say, A tightwad is lower than a snake.

Mike Brown too, in his own way, just wanted to share it around. He liked to talk about the Big Picture, but the way Oradell figured it, he was always saying Be Fair, make sure everyone has some.

She started the engine back up, and Lance asked about the hot dogs.

"Well," said Oradell, "I'll tell you the truth, honey. I'm disappointed about this myself. That old place with the good hot dogs is gone, but we can try another place back on the road I saw. It probably has just as good hot dogs. In fact, I bet the man who made the hot dogs at the street car station moved right up there."

"Let's go now."

"I want to take a little drive through the rest of West Fork first," she said, "since we came this far."

She turned down the narrow street that led to the bridge. It wound around, then across the river. The playing fields were muddy, and there were no swings on the playground, but that could have been because it was so early in the spring. The Company Store and the Rialto were boarded up. It was all so quiet. When she left, the mines had been going full force: jobs for everyone, good salaries, exemption from the service if they wanted it. Boom times because of the War.

She looked over at Lance, but of course he didn't know anything was missing. He was thinking about hot dogs.

She reminded herself it was Sunday morning, but the boarded-up stores didn't have anything to do with church. "It's been nine years," she said, "and they goddam stripped the place to nothing." It made her mad, and she wasn't even sure why. She thought of herself as someone who cut bait when the fish weren't biting, but she didn't like the way it was turning out. There had been people working here, and stores. Where did Mr. Rob-the-Cradle Myers and his invalid wife go? What happened to Stiff Johnson? Did Mr. Talkington convince his wife to leave Marion County when the Company Store closed, or did she convince him to move back to Fairmont and work for her Daddy? Not that it had been the prettiest town or the cleanest town, but it had been— the only one of its kind. "Dead as a doornail," she said.

"Loopy's *real* hungry, Ma," said Lance. The one time he got unpleasant was when his stomach was growling.

She reached in her pocket book, where she kept candy bars. All she had was some Juicy Fruit. "Feed that to the little potato sack," she said.

"You said hot dogs."

"Oh shut up Lance," she said. "Chew the gum.

We'll get out of this hole and get you a hot dog in no time at all. Just let me have a look around." She drove up to the mine gates, which were padlocked. "Looky here, Lance, there's where 400 men died in a big explosion. And they say there was a lot more of them, only the rest was little boys, and they didn't count them."

Lance gazed at the crushed coal road. "But you were okay?"

"I wasn't born yet, honey."

It had always been told like a story to her, too. At least it took Lance's mind off his stomach. He said, "Is that a graveyard in there?"

"No, it's a mine. The boy in the filling station said they still work some. It's a bunch of holes and tunnels under the ground where men go and dig out coal. A long long time ago, before I was born, all those men died in there. And one of those men was your great grandfather."

"He died in there?"

"Yeah, but they brought the dead bodies out and buried them somewhere else." She didn't even know where. Some Catholic cemetery somewhere, she supposed. But she didn't know. She didn't know anything about people on that side of her family. There must have been some uncles or aunts or somebody, but she never knew. "But don't you forget!" she said in a loud voice. "Your great grandfather died in a hole in the ground digging to make some rich bosses richer!"

She meant to head straight back for the highway and lunch, but at the bottom of the hill, she turned up Mud Street. It was still unpaved, but the out-houses were gone. "You used to have to go use the pot in a little house out back, Lance, but somebody finally installed plumbing." He laughed, like she was telling a joke. He had been late learning not to poop his pants, which used to drive Harry wild. "No, it's true, Lance. Most people didn't have indoor bathrooms. A few people did. The Talkingtons did."

Halfway up, a lot of the houses had new painted cement porches. Higher up was a little group separated from the others, all fixed up with asphalt siding and new windows and fences and gates. Suddenly, she realized that the best looking one—the one with the newest siding and fresh paint on the trim—was her house.

She stopped the car in the middle of Mud Street. "Look at that," she said to Lance. "That's the house where I lived with your grandpa Hugh Riley. Well, I never expected it to look so good. And they already turned over a vegetable garden. It must be Italians."

Lance said, "What's a Talian?"

"You're partly one," she said. "I mean, I was part Italian, and your old man is half Italian and half a Jew, maybe. I don't think he knows for sure. Anyhow, you got some Italian and some Jewish and some regular American from the Rileys, only they used to say the Rileys had an Indian back there too." Lance liked that. One of his favorite toys, packed away for this trip, was a plastic Indian village in a cardboard box. He leaned forward, pressing on Loopy, listening. "So, anyhow, some people come from this place called Italy, and they were real good at growing gardens."

A woman opened the door and stood behind the screen of the next house over, where the Pierces used to live. Oradell got out and walked up to the little gate, which didn't used to be there. "Good morning," she said.

The woman didn't say a word, but she crossed her arms over her chest. She was white, but she looked as close-mouthed as Mrs. Pierce herself. Oradell pointed. "I used to live in that house next door. I lived there just me and my daddy." No response. "Yeah, and now I've been away almost ten years, living in Las Vegas. I'm moving to Pennsylvania. I'm always saying how friendly people are in West Virginia. Back home, I always say, people can be mean as the devil, but they'll help you out if you need it. My daddy's name was Hugh Riley."

The woman took her time answering. "Never knew him."

Oradell said, "In your house, there was a colored family named Pierce."

The lady answered that quick enough. "No there wasn't. They live out the road in Polkville."

That was the first Oradell heard of the colored community out there getting called Polkville. She said, "The Pierces moved out there?"

"I don't know no Pierces," said the woman. "But they never lived here."

"Well, yes, as a matter of fact, they did. Mr. Pierce was a janitor at the school."

"Well," said the woman, "if they did, they wasn't colored."

This woman is real stupid, she thought. "Listen, did you all just now get plumbing up here?"

"This house always did have plumbing," said the woman. "I swan!"

And slammed the door.

Lance was leaning his head on Loopy, looking mournful.

"Well," she said, "we're on our way, now," and she backed into the woman's driveway and spun some gravel on her way out. She meant to go straight over the river and out of there forever and find Lance a hot dog, but, again, it was as if the Ford knew better than she did where she wanted to go. It turned up the alley just before the bridge, Grace Howard's street.

"Well, Lance," she said. "Since we're here, we'll try one more place."

"I'm awful hungry," he said.

"Oh, you're just bored. If this friend of Mommy's is home, she'll give you a cookie." These houses looked to be in pretty good shape too. It seemed to be mostly the businesses that had closed down. She pulled over at the wide spot by Grace Howard's garage. They went up the back walk to the screened back porch at Grace's house, Lance dragging Loopy, chewing his gum. Oradell didn't think she had ever gone to the front door. Now who's going to live here, she wondered, stepping in past some worn down brooms and a milk can someone had painted green. She tapped at the kitchen door.

Grace Howard came. There wasn't any preliminary noise, just all of a sudden the storm door opened, and there was Grace with her big round face, lower than it used to be. She was wearing an old fashioned pinafore apron, and she peered over her glasses said. "Well, good Lord God in Heaven, it's Oradell Riley."

Oradell was so grateful she had to watch out not to cry. "It's me," Oradell said, "and this here is my little boy Lance." And she pulled him around, as if she had come all this way just to show off her little boy.

Grace said, "My my. How old is he?"

"How old are you Lance? Tell the lady? This is Mrs. Grace Howard. Take that gum out of your mouth, honey."

She reached in his mouth and got the gum, kept it in the palm of her hand. Lance raised five fingers on the hand that wasn't holding Loopy.

"He's big for five," said Grace. "He's almost as big as you, Oradell. You're just as little as ever."

Lance whispered, "Loopy's hungry, Mommy."

And of course, Grace stepped right aside and let them in. "Git that child in here, Oradell," she said. "Let me give this child something to eat. Throw the gum in the trash over there. He looks like he needs some lunch. Are you traveling and you didn't carry sandwiches for the child?"

Grace made it easy for people. That was the kind of person Grace was. The thing was, the reason Oradell had always been half mad at Grace, was that she felt like Grace could have made everything right all along. She felt like Grace could have been her mother, if she'd tried. Maybe even saved Mike.

Grace's kitchen was the first thing to look really familiar. There were waves in the linoleum, and the colors grayed and yellowed, but it was still the same old-fashioned kitchen with a big white enamel table where Grace used to line up Ball jars for canning. The stove was the first gas stove Oradell ever cooked on. There was a wooden God Bless This House plaque made by one of Grace's boys.

Grace settled Lance at the table on a yellow stool and talked about her neighbors. Did Oradell remember this one and that, and how would Lance like some French toast?

I would like that very much, he said.

Well, good, said Grace, and offered the bathroom, which Oradell didn't really need, but she went anyhow, just to see if there was still a crocheted cover in the shape of an old fashioned lady's hat over the spare toilet paper. And there was: lavender. The old one had been green and white.

Before going back to the kitchen, she took a look around the living room, dark and crowded with furniture. The windows gave out on the bright yellow morning, and the river and muddy playing fields below. She didn't go in the front bedroom where she had labored with the Baby.

Grace was talking to Lance about food while she made French toast. Oradell asked about Grace's family, and Grace told her where her kids were and how Mr. Howard died of a heart attack. Oradell was sorry for that. He had been a nice man, always working: his shift at the mines, then in the garden, then in the garage fixing things. Grace's girls were all married, of course, one all the way in Michigan. "I hate that so bad," said Grace. "I never liked people being so far away they can't come by and see you."

She means me too, thought Oradell.

Grace's son lived on the other side of the county, on a farm. "He got a job at the Westinghouse factory," said Grace. "He'd like to be a farmer, but you can't make a living at that. And you know Oradell, the mines have slowed down a whole lot, and it's hurt people, but I'll tell you the truth, I don't care because I never wanted any of my family down there anyhow." Grace slid two nicely browned French toasts onto Lance's plate.

"I thought you'd be in church," said Oradell.

"They don't need me at church," said Grace.

"I thought by now you'd of turned into one of those praying fools."

Grace narrowed an eye at Oradell over her glasses. "I've done my time, and the Lord knows my heart. I keep busy with this life and trust Him to take care of the next one." She brought Lance the syrup and a glass of milk and cut up his French toast into bite sized pieces.

"Thank you," said Lance. "Loopy thanks you too."

"He's a real polite child," said Grace. "You're doing a good job with him. How many pieces do you want, Oradell?"

She opened her mouth to say none, thanks, but she said, "Oh, I wouldn't mind one or two."

Grace started to make Oradell's. Grace's face was toward the stove when she said, "Where've you been anyhow, Oradell? I guess the post cards got lost in the mail."

"I never sent any."

"That's what I thought."

"I didn't think it mattered to you, where I was. You had so many of your own."

Grace was heating coffee, had four slices of bread in the pan now, sprinkled on a little cinnamon. "How is that stuff?" she asked Lance.

"It's *good*," said Lance. "It's *real* good."

"Well you can have all you want," she said. "Poor little thing, his mama don't hardly feed him."

"You can tell that all right," said Oradell, and they both smiled at Lance's big arms and big shoulders and round pink cheeks.

Grace said, "You know, Oradell, I always felt like you were something to me. I mean, I had my own children and all that, but you always turned up here when you needed something—"

"Only if I had to."

"That's what I mean. You came to me when you needed mothering. That's why it felt like you were one of mine. Why, I would have taken you in a minute, Oradell, but first there was your hardheaded father who wouldn't allow it, and then you were just as hard headed."

Oradell had to force it out, but she managed to say, "You took me in when I needed it most. I don't suppose I ever said thank you."

"No, I don't suppose you ever did."

"Well, I'm saying it now. Thank you."

"You're more than welcome, Oradell, honey. Mostly I'm just glad to see you looking so good. I used to worry about you."

"Well, I made some mistakes, but I'm doing okay. I'm on the express track now."

Lance said, "I don't mind if I do," even though no one had offered him anything.

Grace pursed her lips to keep back a smile and slipped two of the fresh French toasts onto his plate and cut them up. Grace never laughed, but she had a sense of humor. She would tell stories with this long, mournful face on, and never crack a smile, but everybody else would be in stitches. She put Oradell's French toast in front of her and poured coffee.

Oradell had a choked feeling in her chest and stared at the food. "I suppose I should have asked first— I mean, I came to see you, Grace, and to show you Lance. But I wanted to know, whatever happened to— you know—"

"The baby?"

Grace and Oradell both looked at Lance. He was offering a bite to Loopy. He didn't seem to be paying any attention.

"I always wondered what you expected to happen to her, Oradell, the way you left."

Oradell felt a thickness in her mouth, "I should have left some of the money they gave me for Mike. To help take care of her. I was just a kid—I wasn't thinking very straight."

"I know you were just a kid. That's why nobody's mad at you, but I wondered. Did you think she'd be sitting here playing with her dolls, waiting for you to come by and pick her up?"

Oradell had probably been imagining something just like that.

Grace said, "The answer to your question is, she's doing fine, Oradell. She isn't here, and I was glad to do what I did, but you should have at least sent her a Christmas card."

"I didn't come down here to have you tell me what I did wrong."

"Little boy," said Grace. "I see you're finished with those French toasts. If you walk straight in through there, to the front, you'll find a big basket full of toys under the window. I keep them for my grandchildren." He picked up Loopy and went into the living room, and Oradell ate two bites of her French toast, which was very tasty, considering everything. Grace refilled her own coffee and Oradell's, and then said, "Well, the short version of it is, we found a nice Christian couple who couldn't have children and always wanted a child. He was a preacher from Green County, Pennsylvania."

"A preacher!" said Oradell.

"Then he got a church down near Atlanta, Georgia. Somewhere around there. I can give you their address and I can show you the pictures they send me every year at Christmas. I would have kept her for my-self, but this couple was so crazy about her. Do you want to see the pictures?"

"I should have stayed," said Oradell. "I shouldn't have let that baby go."

"Well, then you wouldn't have that sweet little boy in the other room, honey. Look at it that way."

"I left his father. We were married and all, but he wasn't worth much. I'm doing okay."

"Do you want to come and see those pictures?"

"Yes," said Oradell. "Please."

"I keep one old one in my pocketbook," said Grace, "but I have most of them in the front bedroom."

Lance had taken out some blocks and trucks from the grandchildren basket. The front bedroom was as Oradell remembered it, with more of Grace's crocheting, the upright player piano stacked with baskets and shoe boxes and cigar boxes. The bed pushed over to one side now, out of the way. "I never meant to stop by today, Grace," said Oradell. "I goddam meant to drive right on—"

"You still cussing, Oradell?" said Grace.

The thing about Grace was that while she didn't approve of cussing, she never made it feel like she didn't approve of Oradell.

"Oh, Grace, you know me," said Oradell. Saying those words, just to be able to say those words, made her feel so good. She was always meeting people who didn't know her at all. It would have been too bad to come back to West Fork and not see anybody who knew her. "You know me. I guess I was always a diamond in the rough and I guess I always will be." Grace was slowly moving some shoe boxes, looking for what she wanted.

She had moved slow even when Oradell first knew her. "You taught me how to sew skirts, Grace. You were the first one to give me a Kotex." Oradell had been going around with bloody clothes fighting the kids who teased her until Grace said, Oradell, Get yourself in this house and let me tell you a thing or two.

"Here's that box of pictures," said Grace.

It was a cigar box with lots of gold decorations. Oradell went cold all the way through, wanted to bolt, the way you feel when the dentist calls you in. "Grace," she said, as much to put off looking as anything else, "Grace, I can never repay you—"

"You sit in that chair there, Oradell," said Grace. "You sit on the chair and I'll show you these pictures in order." Grace handed them to her one at a time. "This is the picture we had taken for the people when they were inquiring about adopting her," said Grace. It was a professional picture, tinted. A baby with dark eyes like Mike's and its hair brushed up and tied with a ribbon in three places and a little plaid dress fluffed out around it.

"When this picture was taken, I was already gone," said Oradell.

"Now these next ones are what the family took and sent to show us how she was doing." Some snapshots, some studio pictures. Holding a big stuffed Minnie Mouse doll, wearing pink nylon ruffles. Oradell especially liked the one of the baby in a cowgirl outfit and braids.

"They went all out with their pictures, didn't they?" said Oradell.

After a couple of years, there was a second baby with dark hair, another little girl.

"Where'd they get the sister?"

"I don't know, honey. I don' t know if they had a baby or adopted her. I don't know much about their business."

Oradell said, "I never signed any papers, you know."

Grace said, "Oradell Riley, if I thought for one second you would do anything to bother that family, I wouldn't even give you their name, so help me God."

"Oh, I'm not going to bother them, Grace. I can barely make a living for me and Lance. I'd like to send her a Christmas present, though, one of these days."

In the latest pictures, from the year just past, the girl was still bright eyed and smiling with pretty dark hair, but getting leggy. "She's got Mike Brown's smile," said Oradell.

She took the address and the most recent picture and the earliest one. She memorized the name, and the town near Atlanta, and the church where the man was a preacher. And then she stood up, and Grace stood up, and suddenly they were hugging, and Grace said in her deep throat, "Well, love its little heart," and Oradell felt herself getting all gushy.

After that, she always sent Grace Christmas cards and photos of Lance. Grace sent cards that said this was aching and that was aching, and a new address once when the baby's family had moved. Grace died in 1967, and Oradell was always sorry she never went back to see her again, but at least she had finally sent some post cards.

Not once, though, did Oradell send anything to the baby.

Many times she bought gifts and then lost her nerve after counting on her fingers and figuring the baby must be too old for that kind of toy now, or too rich to want a little bit of cheap jewelry like that. Something always stopped her. Sometimes, though, out of the blue, she would start thinking about the baby and how old it would be right now.

She's as old as I was when I first met Morris, she said to herself standing on the deck of the *Golden Argonaut*, looking at the jungle passing by the sides of the Panama Canal.

How can that be?

- 16 -

*O*radell went to lunch after she called Lance. It was the first time she had been to lunch this entire cruise, and the dining room was almost empty. She supposed the people were all out looking at the Canal, or maybe nobody ever came to lunch. The only people at her table were Bill and Cathy Weston in white shorts with pastel polo shirts, lime green for Bill, peach melba for Cathy.

As she took her place, she said, "Surprised to see me?"

"Yes," said Cathy. "I'm surprised. Are you surprised, Bill?"

Bill was sitting with his body angled slightly away from the table, reading. He closed the book over his fingers. It was a Louis L'Amour western. He stared over his reading glasses at Oradell, but didn't speak.

"So you're a reader, are you, Bill?"

Bill grunted and shrugged, went back to the book. Nikko came out of the kitchen. That was good news for the Westons, if they only knew. Oradell surprised herself by feeling relieved to see him, as if, push coming to shove, she didn't want anything going on between him and Tracy. But I don't care, she thought. None of my business. I did my bit for humanity in the middle of the night last night.

"He always reads Westerns," said Cathy. "That's what he does on vacation, Westerns from dawn to dusk."

Bill grunted again. Oradell almost liked him. No nonsense about trying to impress people, just reading his book. Her eyes seemed unusually sharp today: she could see in great detail the lean, powerful cowboy making a lonely last stand on the cover of Bill's novel. She said, "I always was a sucker for cowboys myself. Gary Cooper was my favorite. I always fell for guys who pretended to be cowboys. Where is everybody today? I saw Tracy down at the pool."

"Tracy doesn't come to lunch. Nobody comes to lunch, except us."

"I figured the Blumes for the three-squares-a-day sort of folks."

"They walk around the deck three times instead of eating lunch. I usually order a fruit salad, but Bill likes to get what he pays for, so we come to the dining room." Another couple wandered over to a nearby table. Cathy said, "Where did the waiter go? I just saw him. I don't know where he went. It seems quieter than usual today."

"Yeah," said Oradell. "It's the Canal. Everybody goes out on deck and waits for something special to happen because it's Canal Day."

Nikko came out of the kitchen again carrying a big tray. He came to them first, smiling broadly. "It is a pleasant surprise to see you, Mrs. Oradell." He began unloading platters of stuffed avocados.

Cathy said, "We didn't order yet."

"Yes, Missis, shrimp salad in avocado today. Best lunch on the menu."

Bill Weston closed the cowboy over his finger again. "Lunch is supposed to be *à la carte*," he said. "Where's the menu?"

Nikko nodded sympathetically and put Oradell's avocado plate in front of her. "It's beautiful shrimp salad today, Chef's Choice. Wait till you taste it."

Weston took his glasses off and put them in his pocket. "I want to see a menu."

Nikko managed to look at once pained and playful. "I'm sorry, sir," he said. "Just for today, we are having Chef's Choice. Everything back to schedule tomorrow. You see, this is Panama Canal day."

Oradell looked around the dining room. She wasn't sure, because she never ate lunch, but she thought there should be more waiters in the room, even on Canal day. "So Nikko," she said, "what's up? The boys aren't staging a little job action, are they?"

"Job action?" said Weston. "What do you mean job action? This is a cruise ship!"

"Everything is fine, Mrs. Oradell," said Nikko.

"I heard the boys were pretty pissed about one thing and another."

"No, no," said Nikko, "it's just Panama Canal Day, everything goes head over heels today."

Oradell would lay her money that there was some quiet malingering going on. "They ought to get organized," she said. "These boys have been pushed around long enough."

"Pushed around in this cushy job?" Weston looked angrily from Oradell to Nikko, then tossed down his napkin. "We'll see about this nonsense."

Cathy said, "Oh, Bill, eat your shrimp."

"Sure," said Oradell. "I'm just jabbering. It's probably nothing, right, Nikko? Nothing special happening today?"

"You know it, Mrs. Oradell."

Weston stabbed his fork into the shrimp salad. "Goddam it," he said. "I don't like this kind of treatment."

So Oradell didn't like Weston any more. Too bad. He should have been a cowboy instead of one of the self-righteous wealthy.

Nikko went on to the next table. "Good afternoon," he said. "This is a very special day, Chef's Choice day, a delicious shrimp salad in avocado for lunch."

"It's good," said Oradell. "Nikko was right about that. They know how to put out a meal on the *Golden Argonaut*, don't they?" When neither Cathy nor Bill spoke, she answered herself. "Yeah, they sure do. They used to have happy waiters too, before this Reese started making trouble."

Bill Weston gave a harumphing noise and ate most of his shrimp salad rapidly, then turned away and began to read again. Cathy ate more slowly at first, then picked up momentum, stabbing two, three, four shrimp on her fork and shoving them in all at once. When her cheeks were fat with food, tears started to trickle down her cheeks.

Bill kept reading.

Yes, Oradell was definitely seeing too clearly today. A clump of wet mascara on Cathy's lower eyelash. "How about a roll, honey? They're awful good."

Cathy shook her head.

Oradell ate the roll and drank some iced tea. "Things do seem a little head over heels today."

Cathy closed her eyes. "You don't know."

Bill snapped his book closed. "I'm going to this Canal thing now," he said, "since everyone's making such a big deal about it. Are you coming, Cathy?"

Cathy shaded her eyes with one hand. "I'll come out later. I think I'll just sit here for a while now."

"Suit yourself."

Oradell and Cathy were the last people in the dining room, and there was not a single waiter in sight. Cathy played with her silverware and cried silently. Oradell said, "Hey, Cathy, I have an idea. You look like you need something to settle you down. Let's you and me take these water glasses and pour the water back in the pitcher and save the ice."

Cathy sobbed a little harder, shoulders jerking up and down, but she still managed not to make any noise.

So Oradell went ahead and dumped the water from both glasses. "Then what we'll do is, we'll take our ice over to the little bar, and I think there's still some calming influence in the cabinet. We'll sit down in private and you can tell old Oradell all about it."

Cathy kept sobbing.

"Come on, Cathy," said Oradell. "Here, you carry the glasses." She shoved them at her, and Cathy took them and got up. She had long, athletic strides, but stumbled several times, and for a change it was Oradell helping someone else walk. "Here, here," said Oradell, puffing slightly, touching Cathy's elbow to navigate her across the dining room and corridor.

The little bar was unlocked, but the shades were down and the bottles put away. She sat Cathy at the glass-topped table that had always been her own favorite, and went around the bar. There was a small padlock on the door of the cabinet.

Cathy buried her face in her arms and started to sob aloud now.

"You go right ahead," said Oradell. "The shades are down, nobody will see a thing. You just relax and cry. I'm going to make an adjustment on this cabinet."

There was a big glass ashtray on the bar. It took two hands to lift it, but she scooted it to the edge of the bar, aimed at the lock, and let gravity pull it down and whack the padlock. "No contest," said Oradell, when it sprang open. And yes, Stavros had left a couple of bottles: rye, scotch, vodka, and Tanqueray. She took the gin to the table and poured one for herself, one for Cathy, and set the bottle on the table between them.

"I should have broken in here a long time ago," she said. "This was my favorite bar, and they closed it. It doesn't even make good sense. It slows things down, not using it. They're fouling things up good this cruise, that Company man Reese. Drink up now, honey."

Cathy knocked back the gin and said, "Brr!"

"Like a pro!" said Oradell. "Have another?"

"Yes, please." Cathy had stopped sobbing, but the tears were still streaming.

"I like pouring drinks for people," said Oradell. "I should have gone to bartending school. That's another one of those missed opportunities. When I was first in New York, when Lance was just a little kid, there was a restaurant where I was working, and they needed a bartender, and they would have sent me to school at their expense. I don't remember why I wouldn't go. I didn't want to be away from Lance the extra hours and women didn't mix drinks so much back then." She glanced at Cathy, who had knocked back another and extended her glass for more. Oradell said, "I don't know, I probably had some boyfriend I thought was the greatest thing since sliced bread. My divorce from Harry the Ape was coming through. I was going to marry the new guy and not have to work. You're dumb when you're young. Who knows. But it was a lost opportunity.

I would have been a great bartender, I like schmoozing. I could have run a restaurant, too. Back when I had my energy. But I never had the dough. I probably never would have got it all together anyhow. Lots of lost opportunities. But look here, Cathy, I don't think you have to worry about Tracy. Kids that age, they'll break your heart, but that's like, part of their job description, you know what I mean? She wants to experience things, she wants to be in love. But she's also very smart, pays attention to the world. In this day and age, even a mistake with a man, it's not the same as it was when you and I were girls. She'll be just fine."

"Tracy?" said Cathy. She had sat up very straight, and Oradell was pretty sure the wet paths on her cheeks were old ones. She hiccuped. "Tracy's fine."

"Yeah, that's what I said."

"Tracy is a good girl. She just doesn't want us to know that."

"Ain't that the way with kids."

Cathy leaned forward. "But really, Tracy is the smallest part of it. It's how we are together. Our family's dysfunctional." She took a big suck of breath and leaned her head back against the plate glass. "I had cancer. I've done well, extremely well, remarkably well. I didn't even have to have the whole operation. Just a lumpectomy."

Oradell blinked and held onto her drink. Conversations about breast cancer always made her want to go into the next room. "That's tough all right."

Cathy tapped a long finger down on the table. "But just the same, it was still cancer! It was an operation! And they didn't even notice." This time she poured her own drink, eyes brimming tears and flashing at the same time. "Did you see how Bill marched off when

I started to cry in there? Like he didn't even see me? That's what they're both like. We're all alike, I suppose. But the day after I got home from the hospital, Bill asked me if we could still host his partner's wedding supper. It was the man's fourth marriage!"

"I hope you told him to go to hell."

"I don't know why I'm telling you this. You don't know Bill. I wasn't surprised. Not a bit."

"You didn't tell him to go to hell, did you?"

"No, of course not. I had said before the operation that I wanted everything to be just the same when it was over. So we did the party. There was some big fight over who was being invited to the supper and who would come and who wouldn't. And then Tracy announced she was quitting school and Bill's doctor's office called to say his prostate was enlarged, and here I was two days out of the hospital, and I just burst out into tears. And they didn't see me. It was like everything was falling apart. It was like my family, like my family—was dis—dis—"

"Functional?"

"Disintegrating." She started to cry again, and this time, instead of filling her glass, Oradell patted her hand.

"Now here's a funny thing," said Oradell. "When I met you folks, I thought it was all Tracy. I thought Tracy was the reason you were on this cruise. See how a person gets things all wrong?"

"I have a dream sometimes," said Cathy, "about everyone turning into sand? They run through my fingers. Then I start turning into sand too. It starts with my feet, and I try to ignore it, but I have trouble walking. Then I'm down on my knees because I don't have legs anymore, and I see my hands, in front of my face, turning into sand too."

Oradell didn't like that sand. She had a vague memory of reading in a magazine about the universe, that if you said the solar system was the size of a grain of sand, and you took all the sand in the world, every grain in the Sahara and Death valley and the beaches in Acapulco and Aruba and San Juan—all of it—and spread it out flat, it would still not be not as big as the universe. She said, "My dream is about this thing crowding me, and there's no room to breathe."

"I tried so hard to make it all right," said Cathy. "To have everything the very best quality, things that wouldn't break or tarnish."

"I never expected for my whole life to be—" Oradell hesitated, looking for what she wanted to say. "So small. You'll think that's funny, someone like me. But when you're a kid, you think what happens to you is huge. Not necessarily good, but important. And now it's like I see it's all so little, even when I help out with something, it's just a little thing."

"You think you have things under control," said Cathy.

Oradell said, "I had a baby. I was a kid Tracy's age, and I had this baby and I ran out on it. But then, you just live on. It was a big thing to me, but not to anyone else. You're not a criminal. You just made a mistake. I should wear a sign on that says what I did, but no one cares. It's like treading water for sixty years, you know? But you keep treading, because if you stop, you drown."

"One minute," said Cathy, "everything is humming around you, the dishwasher is on, the girl has the vacuum running upstairs, there's a load of underwear on Fine Lingerie in the washing machine, and you see that they've come on time for a change to clean the pool, and for a moment, just a moment, it seems like everything is okay, and then the phone starts to ring:

Tracy never showed up at school, the doctor's office says the biopsy results were bad, Bill calls and doesn't even give me time to tell him about the biopsy, he's yelling to cancel the pool cleaner, fire the maid, he just lost a lot of money—"

Oradell shook her head. "I used to think people like you always made up your troubles."

"We're going to be fine," said Cathy, staring into Oradell's face with drunken intensity. "It isn't that we won't make it through. My prognosis is excellent. Bill's business perked up, and his prostate is just a little enlarged."

"But here's what I don't get. If we're all in trouble half the time, why don't we see that the other guy is too? Why doesn't Asshole Reese see what he's doing to the waiters? You know what I mean?"

"I wish Tracy would tell me what's going on with her," said Cathy. "I understand more than she thinks. Of course it isn't like I talked to my mother."

"My mother died," said Oradell. "She died when I could barely walk, and my dad, bless his soul, took care of me as best he could, but he and I didn't know nothing from nothing."

"I was too protected. I yearned to live, but when real things happened, I always started to cry."

"Nothing prepares you for what happens. You can be protected or you can be on your own, but you're not prepared."

"Still," said Cathy, "it would have helped if someone would have talked to me."

"I was two and a half damn years old when my mother died."

"Poor baby," said Cathy.

"Damn straight poor baby!" Oradell realized that she was drunk too. "We'll be okay. I mean, none of us are important enough to get in big trouble."

Cathy had lowered her head. She looked like she was trying to figure out what they were talking about, or else trying to stay awake.

"Well," said Oradell, realizing that at least she had succeeded in distracting Cathy from her sobs. "Well, I guess I'll go take a nap. I didn't sleep so much last night. You ought to go take a nap too."

Cathy lifted her face, heaved her chin up. "No, it's time to go look at the Canal. Bill wouldn't want me to miss the Canal."

As Oradell walked back to her room, she kept a hand on the wall for balance. She was glad she had had the drink with Cathy, and glad she helped out with Jaime in the end. But it didn't seem like enough.

– *17* –

*S*he didn't go to dinner that night. She wasn't feeling well. She was short of sleep. Short of sleep was nothing new, of course. She always used to be short of sleep when Morris was alive. Morris would call her at 5 a.m. because he was awake and worried about his bowels or his breathing, or he wanted to go take a piss and was afraid he'd fall. She'd help him stand on his narrow white old feet with their too long yellow toenails. "I'm not your goddam nurse, Morris," she'd say, and Morris would snap, "You're my goddam whatever I say," and of course he was right because he was paying. She was his nurse when he needed a nurse, his sex partner when he got up enough energy for sex. Most of the time she was his companion and secretary, dispensing his medicine, making his doctor appointments, getting him there on time and having lunch afterward. It wasn't bad. She kept his pills organized, and she knew which ones with food and which ones on an empty stomach.

They had fun spending his money, but she also stuck with him because he was old and sick, and because his sharp gaze would suddenly widen with terror when he thought about dying. When she wasn't feeling well, she wondered who was going to stick with her.

Morris used to have a little secret. He was so scared about dying that he collected pamphlets from religious fanatics and made Oradell read them to him. He figured since she wasn't Jewish it was less humiliating. He would pick apart the fanatics' logic, just the way he picked apart Oradell's, but Oradell knew he was always hoping there might be one that would convince him. He made Oradell swear to destroy all the *Watchtowers* and the rest so his kids would never know. The only pamphlets she ever saw him turn down were the ones from the Lubavitcher Mitzvah tank with its loud speaker and young men in beards and black hats: they made him mad.

"Jews aren't supposed to go out on the street yelling about their religion!" he said. "That's not Jewish!" And if one of them approached him, he'd wave his arms and shout: "Leave me alone! Go away! You got no right to know my religion! If you're so religious, go home and pray!"

"They act like the *goyim*," Morris fumed, "handing out pamphlets!" He liked his pamphlets to be genuine Christian pamphlets: Repent! Do you know Jesus?

"Yes, I know this Jesus," he would say, "Jesus was a good Jew, he never meant to start these trashy religions. Did you know that? I read an article. Jesus wanted to make good Jews, not start all this nonsense."

But just the same, he kept his end-of-the-world pamphlets in a box in his desk, and when he was in the hospital for the last time with oxygen and tubes stuck in every part of him, he beckoned Oradell near and whispered, "Get rid of the Jesus books, you know what I mean? Nobody should know."

She burned them in the fireplace they never used. Morris was right, because his children accused him of being crazy, accused Oradell of hypnotizing him. The greedy bastards. They got plenty too. She was kept busy for a year hanging onto what Morris gave her. His kids hired a lot of expensive lawyers, but Morris's lawyers were more expensive. The judge finally shrugged and said, Listen, there's plenty, you take some, give her some. She never understood people begrudging each other a share.

That was from Mike: Make them share, fight for your share. That was the religion Mike taught her. Mike had been her religion, and when she lost him, she was like one of these Catholics who lose their faith and then tell jokes on the Pope.

She napped through dinner and Stavros around eight-thirty. He brought her a chicken sandwich and orangeade. He took her vodka bottle out of the refrigerator. "Just a little," she said. "I want to taste the orangeade. I always loved the way they make orangeade on the *Golden Argonaut.* Do you boys drink it too?"

"The waiters eat the same as the guests, Mrs. Oradell."

"How about the boys down under?"

"They eat fine."

He leaned over her, gently placed his hands on her ribcage and shifted her upright, plumped her pillows. "I'm not sick, Stavros," she said, but immediately felt weak and wondered if maybe she was. He put the tray on her lap. "You don't have much of an odor, Stavros."

"I got a special deodorant."

She grunted. "It's quiet tonight."

"They all went off at Cristobal."

"I went out one time at Cristobal. The thing about Cristobal is, there's nothing there." She remembered stepping out into the tropical night ready for adventure, and then seeing soldiers at every intersection, keeping you off the side streets. She supposed the General didn't want a lot of American tourists lying bleeding on his streets, but the tourists always felt that their rights had been violated because there was nothing to buy but trinkets made in Southeast Asia. "It's a dump," she said.

Stavros looked like he was about to leave, so she said, "What about Jaime? Did he get off?"

"He's staying on till tomorrow. He'll get off at Cartagena." Then he shrugged. "Mr. Reese watched everyone leave." He asked her if she needed anything else: a slice of cake? She turned him down. He didn't ask if she wanted a man this time, and she hoped that wasn't a bad sign. Her shoulders and head felt heavy, and when he had gone, she finished the sandwich and the orangeade, then leaned back against her pillow with the tray still on her lap.

She had a nightmare of the heavy baby turning into the dead miner. She struggled to wake, barely stopped the tray on her lap from sliding onto the floor.

It was ten o'clock at night and still quiet. The ice had melted in her orangeade. She was going to call Stavros again, but tried to figure out first what she wanted. What she really wanted. To get to San Juan. She could get a doctor's check-up there, she supposed. Not that she was feeling sick, it was this drinking in the afternoon with Cathy Weston, but still you had to wonder about the weakness, the spells. She didn't know if it was enough to make her go to a doctor, though. She used to sit for hours in the emergency room at Pediatrics at St. Luke's Hospital when Lance had asthma. She lost jobs sitting in the emergency room with Lance. Sometimes she thought they were the last poor white people in New York. She used to get panicky, sitting there, with the coughs and limps around her. Sometimes she thought Lance got sick because he needed attention. He used to throw up in the middle of the night, and she'd have to leave her boyfriends, leave work, take him to the emergency room. He was always everyone's favorite patient there, making friends, entertaining smaller, sicker children. He should have been a nurse, she thought.

Morris, of course, had insurance and lots of doctor appointments, but preferred to pay cash from a roll of twenty dollar bills. He said the doctors all used it to buy minks for their wives and diamond bracelets for their girlfriends. They don't pay taxes on half of what they make, he said.

She didn't mind the doctors' offices with Morris. They read magazines, she told Morris a joke, Morris expounded his opinion of doctors in a loud voice.

But she didn't go for herself. She had had her leg broken by a car her second year in New York, and that produced a lawsuit and a few thousand dollars, but the last time she had really been to a doctor was the Wasserman test for marrying Morris. There was the sprained ankle on the *Golden Argonaut*, but she didn't even undress for that. She didn't go to dentists either. She had been to a dentist exactly twice in her life, to have molars extracted. She hadn't gone to a dentist the time Harry hit her in the mouth. Who had the money?

She swallowed a handful of aspirins from the ashtray with the watery orangeade and tried to go back to sleep. There was a tap on her door and a little voice saying, "Oradell? It's me, Tracy."

"The door's open."

"I didn't want to disturb you," said Tracy. She was wearing a white halter top with a flowery full skirt, and she was barefoot.

"Yes you did. Since you're here, you can do me a favor. Take this damn tray and put it somewhere. Stavros usually comes back and gets these things." Tracy put the tray on the chair near the closet and then stood in the center of the room, trying to look sullen. "Why aren't you out on the town? Do you want a drink?"

"No thanks."

"Well, get me my gin out of the refrigerator, will you? Stavros gave me vodka. It's okay in orangeade, but you can't drink the damn stuff straight."

She got Oradell a Tanqueray and then flopped onto the second bed.

Oradell said, "You don't drink, do you?"

"I drink if I feel like it, but I have to have a reason to do things."

"No reason to go out tonight?"

"I did go out. The only interesting thing was some land crabs. They were white with pink claws. I never saw land crabs before, they live in the cracks in the pavement. Where are the people in this town?"

Oradell shrugged. "On the streets where the *turistas* don't go."

Tracy tossed around in the bed, lay on her side, twisted one leg up at an improbable angle and looked at the sole of her foot. "How about the staff? Do they let the ship's staff go on those streets?"

Oradell set her drink aside. "I expect so. The generals usually have investments in the whore houses in these places."

Tracy sat up. "That's what I thought! That's *exactly* what I thought. It's so unbelievable. Nikko had the night off, and it was supposed to be our night. Then all of a sudden, he's like going out with *them* instead of staying with me!"

Oradell said, "I don't know much about lovers' quarrels anymore. If a lover is quarrelsome nowadays, I trade him in for another one."

"This isn't a lovers' quarrel!" Tracy's eyes were filling with tears. "This is about—I mean, I thought this was about—Don't you understand? This was going to be our first real time together. We planned it! He left me to go with—prostitutes! Why did he do this to me?"

Oradell was definitely tired. She definitely didn't feel like going through this again with Tracy. "I expect it hit him all of a sudden, what he was getting into. He's on his own in the world."

"I know he's had to struggle! I know I haven't had to struggle *that* way, but I can imagine. I try to understand. I thought—I thought he understood too. He's on his own because he has to take care of himself physically, but I'm on my own psychologically. No one has any idea what my family is like."

"I had a long talk with your mother today, and she cried too."

"I'm not crying. What did she say?"

"She said when she had her operation, you and your dad pretended nothing happened."

"That was what she wanted! She always wants everything normal. It's her way of preparing me for a life of perpetual hypocrisy. I kept trying to make her tea and toast and stuff, but she wouldn't let me do a thing! Our family is totally—"

"Dysfunctional, yeah, I know."

"What I'm trying to say is, emotionally I'm on my own too."

"Tracy, it's pretty straight up. If Nikko gets caught banging a teenage passenger, he loses his job."

"I wouldn't tell. I would never tell, and even if he did get fired, he ought to be doing something better. I suppose you think that's condescending of me, don't you? You're saying that it's a money thing, what stands between him and me. But I say, being poor doesn't mean you can break your promise!" Tracy had that look again, the raised chin and wide eyes like she was having a religious experience. "You're trying to say that he and I are so different, it will never work. Well, I refuse to accept that."

"No," said Oradell. "I'm not saying that. For all I know, you and Nikko are going to get married and you'll move to Greece and cook his couscous and goat meat for him. I don't know what's going to happen. I'm just telling you why he went out with the boys tonight. He's scared."

"Then I have to give him courage."

"You could also leave him alone. I don't know what you're in such a rush about."

"You're saying I have to give him space. To figure it out for himself."

"I'm not saying anything. I stopped talking."

Tracy came and knelt beside Oradell's bed. "You're telling me it isn't going to be easy. I'm ready for that. I know life isn't going to be easy."

"Nobody knows how hard their life is going to be. Whether you're rich or poor, it's hard, and you end up tired. Listen, Tracy. I'm not feeling so well tonight,

I'm tired, and what I want to tell you is, the main thing is not to get hurt. To protect yourself. You don't want to end up pregnant or picking up some goddam disease."

Tracy smiled and leaned nearer. "Really, I won't. I'm very well educated in that stuff."

Oradell closed her eyes. She thinks because she passed the Condom Quiz she knows about sex.

She felt Tracy's fingertips on her cheek. It made her face go still, as if it were a huge suspended thing, a leather moon, and the soft finger tips reaching to her across space. She was afraid.

"Do you like me?" whispered Tracy, her sweet breath tickling Oradell's ear and neck.

"Oh stop it, Tracy. I don't spend time with people I don't like." The trouble with the touch, Oradell realized, was that it made her want to cry. She said, "I don't have what you want, Tracy."

Tracy whispered, "Tell me about the first time for you and Mike Brown."

"I don't remember."

"Please?"

Tracy's smell was a little perfume, mostly heathy brown and pink skin.

"I remember how he smelled," Oradell said. "That's all I remember. His smell made me happy."

"Oh," whispered Tracy.

But you can't tell an odor, thought Oradell. She remembered being in the house with him, her little house where she had lived with her father, and then alone, and then with Mike, and one warm day, it had seemed to her the whole room was filled with this sweetness rising from the back of Mike's neck, and she had kissed him there. He was doing something else, reading the newspaper or writing a letter, and he reached back with both hands and grabbed her head and shoulders and just pulled her upside down and over onto his lap and held her. That wonderful tumble, to be enveloped in his rich sweetness.

She said, "How could I tell it, Tracy? It's not in words. We were in the middle of the universe. Every move he made, I made the same move and never knew how. I don't have any way to tell you, honey."

"Was it in your little house where you lived with your father, your first time with Mike?"

"Yeah, we were in the shack."

"Was it spring or summer? Did he start or did you?"

"He would never have started. He was trying to take care of me. He thought he was being some kind of hero not to sleep with me, but I kept touching him. I put my hands on him all the time. I leaned on him. I panted and sniffed him like a little bitch hound dog. I wouldn't leave him alone."

"He was in the chair and you were standing?"

"Come on, honey, leave me something just for myself."

"But you do remember it, don't you? It's all right in your head."

"In my chest and stomach."

"I want that, Oradell," said Tracy.

Tracy finally left, and Oradell napped again without turning off the lights. She made up some little dreams with Mike in them. In one, she danced on a picket line and shouted slogans, and Mike came out of the shadows and reached for her, the way she always imagined a movie lover reaching out *and he gathered her in his arms* the way she imagined it even when she had been sleeping with men for years and sometimes liking it and sometimes disgusted with it but never having been *gathered in his arms* except in the movies, in her imagination. And now in this dream, Mike was laughing and pulling her towards him like gathering the waist of a skirt, pulling up the strings that ruffled and smocked her and then his hands and face pressed into her fabric, and she was spreading out, rising in billows in a way she hadn't felt in years.

She came fully awake reluctantly. Knocking at her door again, and the door opening, and it was Stavros.

"Mrs. Oradell," he said, "I didn't mean to come to you. I know you said last night and that was all. I know you did your part already, but the boys are all out, and Reese, he's got all the officers going through rooms. They're looking for Jaime again."

Oradell was still in the propped up position, and her hands were lying in front of her on the outside of the covers. "I was asleep," she said. "I was dreaming."

"You hide him one more time, Mrs. Oradell?"

She hadn't expected to be called on in this way. She had expected that if she was going to help, she would choose when.

"He's here," said Stavros. "There isn't much time." When she didn't say anything, he stepped back, and Jaime came in. Stavros had to go, and then it was Jaime standing in her room staring at her. His eyes round and angry.

"What are you mad about, Jaime?" said Oradell. "I'm the one with my sleep disturbed."

He made a kind of snarl.

"Oh sit down, Jaime," she said. "Get yourself a drink."

He sat on the other bed, where Tracy had sat, but he didn't do anything else.

She thought she would just go back to sleep and forget about him when she heard sounds in the corridor.

Already? she thought. Isn't this too soon?

The noise was a few doors down, a peremptory knock and voices, then doors. She was pretty sure those people had gone out. Were they using keys? Going into passengers' rooms?

After a while, there was the brisk knock on her door. It occurred to her that they would push on in, so she shouted out, "I'm coming! I'm coming! Hold your horses!"

She hadn't been out of bed in hours, and her head swam when she stood up. She touched her finger to her lips to Jaime and gestured at her closet. Her thighs were shaky too. She took her time. Her knees were okay. I'm not afraid, she thought, not this time.

They banged again, and she shouted, "Goddam it, don't rush me! I'll be right there goddam it!"

Jaime moved quickly to the closet, slipped in, pulled it closed. She kept one hand on the bed, then reached for the upholstered chair, the bureau, the wall, finally the bathroom door. "Who's goddam knocking on my goddam door?" she shouted. She realized she had to pee, too. She had been in bed for hours.

There was whispering out in the hall, then someone knocked again, not so loud.

"Who is it?" said Oradell.

"Mrs. Greengold?" The voice was thin and tight even through the door. "This is James Reese, Mrs. Greengold."

"Who's goddam James Reese goddam it? It's the middle of the night."

"I'm sorry to disturb you. James Reese with the Company."

Goddam James yellowleg scab prick Reese, she thought. "So? It's still the middle of the night."

She glanced back. No sign of Jaime. The closet would be the obvious place to look for him, but she didn't intend for them to look.

"We need to speak to you, Mrs. Greengold. We're very sorry to disturb you." Yeah, Sugar Lips, she thought. Try to be polite. I know who you are. "We have reason to believe there is a thief at large. We need to speak with you just for a minute."

She spent some time fooling with the lock, glancing back at the beds. He had been sitting on top of the spread, but it looked smooth enough, at least from this distance, at least with her eyes. There were a lot of beverages on the night stand, but they were actually all hers, and no chance to do anything about that anyhow.

She cracked the door. There was a crowd outside: Reese with his twitchy tan moustache; the First Mate, looking apologetic; some young muscle who was new this trip; and Stavros with the housekeeping keys.

She said, "Well, what kind of party is this? Stavros, too. Are you boys doing room inspections?"

The First Mate said, "We're very sorry to disturb you, Mrs. Greengold."

"Everybody's always sorry," she said. "It's amazing how sorry everybody is."

Reese said, "You must realize that disturbing the passengers is the last thing we want to do."

She concentrated on his ugly little moustache. "I don't must realize anything," she said. "Tell me about your thief," she said. "I heard you going into the rooms down the hall. Nobody's there, so you better have your story good in case something goes missing and they accuse you. I've got some jewelry, no stones, only gold. I never did like stones. But nothing of mine is missing."

The First Mate looked pained. He was a younger, less serene version of the captain. "Please, please," he said. "Nobody has said something is missing!"

"I thought you said there was a thief."

The Mate said, "We are only looking for a missing person. The waiter."

Oradell gave him and Reese both the hairy eyeball. "What waiter is missing? And why would you look for a waiter in my room?"

"Jaime Velez the waiter is missing, Mrs. Greengold," said the Mate. "He was your waiter, and we thought—"

"Thought what? Thought I might be keeping him in my room? Did those Westons tell you I'm friendly with the waiters? Who's telling tales on me and the waiters?"

Reese's lips twitched. "We are trying to protect the passengers, Mrs. Greengold. This crew member Jaime Velez is known to be violent—"

"Oh, I remember. He's the one who popped you in the nose! Oh please. Come on, he's just a little temperamental. And he's missing. Well, I say good for him. I hope you don't find him."

"Oh we'll find him," said Reese. "You can't have a lack of discipline on a ship." She opened the door a tiny bit more, to give him a clear view of the beds.

"You know what," said Oradell, "if I see old Jaime around, I'll tell him you're looking for him. It must be damn serious if you're going in the passengers' rooms when they're out."

"No, no," said the Mate.

"We'll do what we have to," said Reese.

A door cracked open across the hall, so there was someone else home. She raised her voice. "Were you going to come right into my room? Is that the way you do things here?"

"Please, please!" said the First Mate, sounding just like Stavros: "No, no, Mrs. Greengold! We just want you to have a wonderful voyage."

She raised her voice even more. "And what is Mr. Reese going to do to me if it turns out I'm hiding Jaime? Are you going to keelhaul me? Because I don't think anything so goddam awful happened. I think Reese caused a lot of trouble for these boys since he came on the ship, and I think he deserves more than a pop in the nose. A couple of days ago I was thinking about popping him one myself!"

Mr. Reese gave a clipped little bow. "If that's what you think, Mrs. Greengold—"

"That's what I think, honey." She spread out, filled the door with her body, with green nightgown, with expensive unbleached lace. Another door opened, and another. More people home than she thought. Oradell shouted, "Howdy, folks! Y'all come on out for the show now! The Company is doing a speed-up on the waiters, and then they'll cut out housekeeping, and next they're going to take away your extra pillows like they did mine!"

The First Mate cried, "Please, please, Mrs. Greengold!"

"That's right!" she shouted. "First day of the cruise, I noticed I was short a pillow, and I said, 'Where's my extra pillow?' and housekeeping tells me 'Company policy is one pillow per passenger.' All the money we're paying, and the Company only allows one pillow per passenger! I say that's a disgrace!"

The Mate said, "Stavros! Immediately, more pillows for Mrs. Greengold!"

Stavros hurried down the hall. Reese made a hissing sound under his moustache and turned on his heel, stormed down the corridor in the opposite direction. The First Mate bowed and apologized to everyone as he passed. The young man with the muscles seemed confused and walked half backward as if he were protecting the rear, maybe his own rear.

Oradell waved three fingers at him, and he waved back.

"Silly ass," she murmured, waving bye-bye. When they were out of sight, she locked her door and took a few minutes to catch her breath. "Okay Jaime, honey." She tapped the closet.

He looked as sullen as ever, but said, "That's two times, Mrs. Oradell. Two times you do for me."

"Just walk me back to the bed, Jaime. I'm a little unsteady. You stay on top of the covers, like you were doing, in case they come back. That Mr. Reese surely don't like me. Well, I don't like him either goddam it. Listen, if you need a blanket they're in the closet— "

"I don't need nothing," said Jaime. "Two times is too much, Mrs. Oradell."

"And I appreciate that you reckanize the obligation. And if you don't get to pay me back, just pass it along and do for somebody else someday, okay? That's the way to do it, keep the good deeds circulating."

She turned off the lights and lay bright and alert, with a strange sensation of seeing in the dark. "Listen, Jaime," she said, "seriously, this guy Reese is nothing but trouble."

"Cartagena," he said. "I got a cousin in Cartagena."

After a while, when she didn't go to sleep, she played her game of imagining it was Mike in the other bed, that she and Mike had had a whole life together.

That he had lived and they had a houseful of kids, and he had gone off from time to time, but he always come back, and when the kids got big, she went with him, and they stood up for the working people.

She imagined that their kids had given them this cruise for an anniversary present. This was the first real vacation they ever had. Mike would be heavier, still bow-legged, full of energy, and he would still have that way of grinning with his whole body.

Jaime made a little bark in his sleep.

She remembered one time the summer she lived with Mike that she had awakened in the middle of the night. It was rare for her to be awake and Mike asleep. Usually she drifted off to the sound of his pen scratching and woke to the smell of coffee in the morning. She had been a pregnant teenager and him a grown man full of important business. But this one fresh smelling night, she sat bolt upright in bed with Mike asleep next to her, under the sheet, just the top of his head visible. She had swelled with sweet protectiveness toward the top of his head, toward his body, and she had imagined she would do anything at all to take care of him.

And then, in the event, hadn't even been able to ask the Bosses what really happened. I wish I could have done something, Mike, she thought. I wish I hadn't of just whimpered and took the envelope of dollars and never even looked in the coffin.

Hell, she thought, I'll never even know if I buried Mike.

- 18 -

The main thing about her first time with Mike wasn't how sexy it was, or how exciting, but how he made her feel like everything connected, that she was part of things she hadn't even known existed. She had smelled him, and gone over and kissed the back of his neck, and he tipped her head over heels and said something like What am I going to do with you, and Oradell wanted him to do everything. And yes he was gentle and yes he wanted her to enjoy it and yes afterwards he told his stories all over again, lying in bed with their arms and chests bare, Mike's arms behind his head, and Oradell amazed at the contrast of pale skin on the underside of his arms and the dark hair in his armpits, and he told it all again, about how the individual person steps over a line to stand with the rest of the people and then you become a part of History.

She dreamed of the Giant Miner when she finally slept. She went to sleep thinking of Mike Brown, but she dreamed of the Giant Miner lying in the street of West Fork, blocking the streets, blocking the mine, blocking the sky, blocking her breath. She was starting to struggle to breathe again, but instead she woke to hear Stavros coming in, taking Jaime out.

She didn't speak to them, just lay there waiting for their dark on dark figures to subside from something terrifying to something ordinary. Then she closed her eyes, when the door clicked, waited for her breath return. And the miner turned into Mike. He was still dead and still enormous, but not as big, and he wasn't choking her. He was not yellow and no dust poured from his nostrils: he was pink and brown skinned like a person, and his eyes were closed and he was smiling. He was dead, but also warm and smiling.

In her dream, there was a huge sigh, relieved and sad. It was her sigh or maybe the dead miner's sigh.

In the dream, she felt a kind of freshness, as of a sky after rain, or an emptied bladder, or crying. She saw Shacky Hill and felt sad that she would never go there again. Felt a sadness in movie colors: ocher, blue, and orange, and the oceanic music of a movie sound track.

The next morning, Oradell stayed in bed. Stavros said, "You didn't eat much Mrs. Oradell."

And she said, "I have a touch of flu or something. One of my spells."

"You want the shade up?"

"Yes. No. I don't know. I'm too tired to decide. Did you all find a place for Jaime?"

"Jaime is fine. I don't know, you don't look good, Mrs. Oradell."

She closed her eyes again. She felt strange, light headed. "I'm tired. Maybe I'm tired of doing what I please."

"They tore up everything again looking for him. This afternoon, we'll be in Cartagena."

"I know, Jaime's got a cousin in Cartagena. And he's going to sneak off today. Good. Do you want to put him in here with me for a couple of hours?"

"You're on our side, Mrs. Oradell. Always on our side."

She didn't think she was strong enough today to be of much use to anyone's side, but she appreciated him saying so.

"You don't even eat your roll, Mrs. Oradell."

"I'll eat it later. Or you could take it away. I don't care."

"Mrs. Oradell? You want to see Dr. Clyde?"

"No, I'm just a little hung over. " She started to get up on her elbow, but the sudden movement sent her head spinning and her stomach heaved. To her surprise, because it happened so quickly, she found herself retching over the side of the bed. Stavros was holding her head, helped her lie back. She was going cold, maybe even fainting. She faded, came back and saw Stavros wiping up the floor, then faded again.

After a space of time, she saw Dr. Clyde's face in front of her.

For a flash she thought it was Dr. Wormley, but knew better and was frightened by her own confusion. His face faded, and when it came back, someone was holding her hands.

Doc Clyde said, "So you haven't been feeling well, Oradell."

"Who told you that?"

He said, "You have a weak pulse. I think we'll have someone meet you at Cartagena."

"I don't know anyone in Cartagena."

"To check you over, make sure everything is A-OK."

"I'm not getting off the ship."

"Just for the day. I radioed ahead."

She was pretty sure that the slide-away grayness and fainting were over for now. Things around her felt squared away. She said, "Radio them again. I'm staying on the *Golden Argonaut*, Clyde." He didn't want her to sit up, but she did anyhow. "I'm better now. I have these spells. They're nothing." It was true, even as she spoke, it was coming back to her, that she had spells, that she was fine between them, and didn't think about them.

"You need a check-up."

"You're probably right. I'll get one when I get home."

"I'd feel better if you had one now."

"San Juan then."

"When they find out in Cartagena that everything is fine, you'll catch up," he said. "You can get back on tonight or if you have to stay overnight—"

"No!"

"—you'll take a plane to Aruba or Caracas and join us there. Just get your check-up first."

They used to sit in the bar together when she first came on the *Golden Argonaut*. He was a gossip, he had been a doctor in the army, and he used to hang out with the Foreign Service crowd in different places around the world. He always knew who was sleeping with who and who drank too much. She didn't like this benevolent bedside manner. "You're treating me like I was about to croak."

He patted her hand. Hers was skinny with rings, his was fat and hairy. "Be my patient for a little while, Oradell."

"You scare me when you're so nice. I'm better."

"I can see."

"I've had these spells for a long time, they're nothing. I get a little queasy and sometimes I faint. A hangover's a lot worse. Maybe this is just a hangover anyhow."

"Umm," said Doc.

"Nothing hurts!"

"Good."

196

"So don't call in the Medics."

"I think you've been neglecting your health, Oradell. You needed a check-up a long time ago. "

"Fine. I'll get one. Call them in Puerto Rico and I'll do it there. I don't want to do it in a foreign country."

"I think you better do it in Cartagena." He said it in that firm, kindly tone that sent a chill through her.

What is it, Doc? a little voice inside her whispered. Is it my heart, Doc? Is it my pressure? Aloud she said, "Whatever they're going to tell me, I don't want to know."

"It's probably nothing, or just a little thing. You're too smart to put your head in the sand about your health when you could maybe take a pill and be fine."

"What the hell gives you the idea I'm too smart to put my head in the sand?"

"Just go to the doctors, get a check-up. You don't even have to stay all day if you don't want to."

After Clyde left, Stavros came back with tea and toast, and she ate it, and felt much better. She asked him what time it was, how long till Cartagena, when were they bringing in Jaime.

"We don't need to hide him here."

"Bring him in, I'm fine. Look at me." Stavros helped her to the bathroom, and she didn't feel faint, so she was pretty sure that the spell was over. The only thing different was that this time, because of goddam Clyde and his beside manner she was remembering all the other spells.

She lay in bed for a while with her eyes closed. After a while, Stavros came back, and she heard him making little noises, straightening up her room. Then the door opened again, and Nikko was with him. They whispered.

"What's up, boys?" she asked.

The two of them: Stavros small and intense, Nikko looming over him with his big shoulders and bright eyes, grinning.

"So Nikko," she said, "did you and Tracy make it up?"

He looked away too quickly, and she thought, She must have waited for him last night. He tried to get out of it, but Tracy got her way.

She said, "What's the plan for Jaime?"

Stavros shrugged, as if it were something of no importance. "Some of them thought we would dress Jaime up in lady's clothes and sneak him out, if we could find a lady to lend the clothes."

"And you two came by to ask if I had any spare dresses? So the plan is what, that he just strolls out?" she said. "Like a tourist? Where is he now?" Her fingers started drumming on the bed beside her. Her fingers were working something out. Her fingers were ahead of her brain.

"He's all right for now," said Stavros. "He's down below."

Her fingers drummed the idea right into her mouth. "Well, how about this one. How about if when they come from that Cartagena hospital to get me, Jaime ends up on the stretcher instead. I'm not going to any goddam Colombian sawbones anyhow."

Stavros frowned. "Dr. Clyde says you need a check-up."

"I don't like doctors. I never would have been so nice to Clyde, if I'd knowed he was a real doctor. I thought he was just another host to drink with the old ladies."

Stavros got her small bag off the top shelf of the closet.

"Why are you doing that?" she said. "I told you I'm not going anywhere."

"Dr. Clyde said to pack you some things. He's a good doctor, Mrs. Oradell."

Oradell sucked her teeth. "He don't know shit from shinola. I'm still here, and I'm still paying."

Nikko said, "We want to make sure you're fine for next time, Mrs. Oradell."

Her fingers kept drumming. "All right, Stavros," she said. "Keep packing the bag. This is how we can do it. We pretend I'm really sick. I'm going to feel so awful that I groan and keep my face covered when they roll me off the ship. I'm going out all wrapped up in blankets and a big robe so no one could see even if I happened to have a five o'clock shadow. Did Jaime shave this morning?"

Stavros and Nikko looked at each other. Stavros said, "Do you really want to do this, Mrs. Oradell?"

"If we were in San Juan, I'd go to the hospital. Once we get to San Juan, I will go. I'll get the whole goddam check-up. But I'm not going to a goddam Colombian witch doctor. I mean that. I'm staying on the *Golden Argonaut* today. So if you want to give Jaime his best shot, do what I'm saying. Let the stretcher come, and he'll go out wrapped up in scarves and whatnot. I've got a wig, now that I think about it, for bad hair days. Stavros, you'll walk alongside and hold the patient's hand, and maybe slip a few American dollar bills to the stretcher boys and the ones who drive the ambulance so that if the patient should happen to feel better and decide to get out and go shopping, nobody squawks."

Nikko cried, "Mrs. Oradell is Saint Angel!"

She said, "It's not like anyone is going to get in trouble. Even if I did get sick tonight or tomorrow, they'll bring in a helicopter and airlift me off the ship. Nobody loses. Everybody wins. Jaime gets to go visit his cousin in Cartagena, you boys get to play a trick on Asshole Reese, and I get blamed if there's any trouble. Who can lose?"

For half a second it occurred to her that she could get banned from the *Golden Argonaut*, they could do that to her, but she shoved it aside. She was like goddam little Tracy: she knew what she wanted. Mike Brown would have been proud of her. He would have organized the boys and changed everything from the bottom up, but this was a different time.

Nikko was grinning, but Stavros kept worrying. Stavros wanted to get Jaime off and also save everyone's jobs. "What about Dr. Clyde? He maybe thinks he's going on the ambulance with you."

It was like that morning in Las Vegas when it had come to her that she was leaving Harry. Everything falling into place. You couldn't throw one at her that she couldn't hit. "Okay," said Oradell. "Let's work on that. We'll make a distraction. One of the boys in the engine room has an asthma attack. No, better. I've got a better idea. Nikko, get your girlfriend in here."

He shook his head, rolled his eyes. Stavros made a sour mouth.

Oradell said, "Come on, Tracy wants to Do Something important. She needs a cause and Jaime needs a way off the ship. She'll eat this up. Go out and get me one of those orangeades and a chicken sandwich and tell Tracy I want to talk to her. How long do we have? We have to figure out something for her to get sick with."

Stavros didn't like it a lot. "You don't want to get passengers involved in this."

"That's a lot of bull, Stavros. You got me already, and you're getting her too."

Nikko said, "I am on my way, Mrs. Angel. I'm always calling you Angel now."

Stavros went out, and Tracy came in, then Nikko behind her with a tray. Tracy said, "Are you okay, Oradell? Everyone is so worried about you." Nikko put the tray on Oradell's lap. Tracy sat on the second bed. They were scrupulous not to touch each other.

Oradell thought the orangeade was especially good today: fresh juice with a little sugar syrup, a spritz of seltzer, and hold the vodka. "I was under the weather," she said. "But I'm still alive, and don't you forget it."

In the end, alive was what you wanted. Not to avoid danger, but to feel alive. Glimpses of truth popped up one after another around her, like ducks in a shooting gallery. Alive was why people loved sex. She looked at the two of them, young lovers, fresh orangeade. Whatever's most alive.

Nikko sat down beside Tracy on the bed, but still not touching. They smiled at Oradell, and she wondered about the scene when Tracy waylaid him as he came back on board. That was their business, hers was with Mike. Theirs together was to get Jaime off the ship without anybody getting arrested. When she got home, Oradell would let Lance send her to the hospital, let them stick the plastic tubes up her nose, needles in her arm. All the tests. Only don't tell me the details in advance.

She said, "We've got a project for you, Tracy. Did you tell her yet?" He shook his head. "Here's the deal.

They've got an ambulance meeting us in Cartagena."

"Oradell! You *are* sick!"

"No, I'm not sick, and I'm not going off on any stretcher. You'd have to be crazy to go to the doctors in Cartagena. Caracas, maybe, but not Cartagena. But just the same, Doc's got an ambulance and stretcher coming to meet the boat. And someone is going to go out on the stretcher. Somebody all wrapped up in scarves and blankets."

"I don't get it," said Tracy.

"Well," said Oradell. "Honey, now you say no if you don't want to do this. This is optional, and we probably shouldn't get you involved. I don't know, Nikko. Should we get her involved?"

"She's so young." He smiled at the ceiling.

"Tell me what's going on!" Tracy was wearing red today, a sundress like a bandana tied behind her neck. The hardest part was going to be convincing anyone that she was sick.

"We're trying to sneak Jaime off the ship," said Oradell. "You know, Jaime the waiter."

"The one who punched Mr. Reese!"

"Jaime says he never made contact, but, yeah, that's the one. And the boys and I came up with a plan. We're going to sneak him off on my stretcher, and we need some help."

Tracy was looking from Oradell to Nikko and back. "On the stretcher that's coming for Oradell? That's so cool!"

Nikko said, "I don't know if we should help Jaime. He's so bad temper. I don't know if he deserves to get help."

"Nikko!" cried Tracy. "This is Solidarity! Right, Oradell? This is someone in trouble and you have to choose which side you're on, right? The bosses or the real people? Right, Oradell?"

Oradell said, "You could also look at it as just helping out an old friend. Or you could look at it as screwing Asshole Reese. There are a lot of ways of looking at it."

Nikko said, "I don't know why Mrs. Oradell wants to help Jaime. She should help me. Give me all her money."

"Shut up Nikko," said Oradell. "The bottom line is, we need Tracy to make it work."

"Me!"

"Yeah, we need someone to distract Doc Clyde so he won't come and try to examine me or do his comforting doctor bit. It has to be a passenger."

"I get it!" said Tracy. "I could faint? Break my leg? I'll pretend to kill myself. I'll bleed. I'll actually cut myself—Wait, I've got it! I'll go hysterical. I'll lock myself in the room and scream that I'm bleeding."

"Not bad," said Oradell, "if the timing's just right."

"Nikko can tell me when to start. He can pretend to hear me screaming. I'm good at screaming if I get in the mood. And, let's see, Nikko, do you think you could get me a bag of, I don't know, cow blood from the kitchen? I could let it run under the door—"

"Skip the bag of blood," said Oradell. "Let's keep it simple. All we have to do is keep Doc occupied long enough for the stretcher boys to get in and out so he doesn't come and check on me."

Tracy gave a little nod and said, "I'll do whatever makes it work best."

Tracy and Nikko kept talking. Tracy had decided it would be food poisoning. Then Nikko had to set up for lunch. Tracy went with him, then came running back into Oradell's room. No, no, it was going to be a suicide attempt!

After a while, Oradell realized she might be feeling woozy again.

After Tracy's third trip back with a new idea, Oradell said, "I'll tell you what, you decide which it's going to be, and I'm going to take a nap."

Tracy said, "I think just screaming without explaining why. I can see how that will work best. I'll check with Nikko to see what he thinks. But in my mind, inside myself, I have to know why I'm screaming."

Oradell slipped in and out of sleep a little longer. She thought she might be feverish. She had feverish dreams, and in one of them Mike Brown came to her. "Standing there as big as life," she said, only she didn't speak aloud, and he wasn't stranding but sitting on the other bed, grinning the way Nikko had grinned at Tracy. Young enough to be her grandchild, or that Joe who tried to get her to organize the grocery store, years ago, everything was years ago now.

Mike sat with his legs open, his hands loose in his lap, short legged, or sitting back too far. In any case, his feet dangled and his brogans didn't touch the floor.

"Your shoes are muddy," Oradell told him.

"I was a miner," he said.

"No you weren't," said Oradell. "You were a Commie organizer."

His grin faded a little as if he were puzzling over something, and then he said, "But I went in there. In the mines." He seemed to fade in and out too, the way Oradell did when she was having a spell.

She said, "You left me in a lot of trouble. I don't mean just pregnant, I mean confused."

He nodded. "I wasn't good on the details."

"Like keeping me from getting pregnant."

He blinked, the grin faded. It seemed to make him fade too, like somehow his image depended on the grin. He said, "I expect I wouldn't be dead if I'd paid attention to the details."

"Shit," said Oradell. "Just think what we could have had if you'd stayed alive."

Here came the grin again. "Aw, Oradell, I'd be dead anyhow from something."

"I suppose," she said. "One way or the other. If not today, tomorrow."

He was fading fast now, and she felt such a pure sadness: how sad to lose him, whichever way. He faded away, and she did too, both of them asleep like the old married people she'd always wanted them to be.

She woke after a little while and thought: Well, well, I had a conversation with Mike in my dream.

The boat engines were reversing, to slow down. They would be coming into port. Stavros arrived with Jaime.

Jaime was glowering. "You keep doing for me and doing for me, Mrs. Oradell!"

"Don't say thank you," she said, and he didn't.

He sat on the bed where Mike had been and shook his head in amazement or annoyance. Oradell told Stavros where the wig was, a big tousled auburn number. She said, "I paid a fortune for that ugly thing a couple of years back. Some idiot gave me a pixie haircut that made me look like a wart hog. But in the end, I decided I looked better as a wart hog."

She sat up in bed again. At least she didn't vomit. Tracy stuck her head in one last time. "I'm just going to scream and lock my door! If Mike Brown was alive, Oradell, he'd be doing this with us."

"Hell, honey," Oradell said, "If enough men like Mike had lived, this shit would never happen."

Jaime was getting lipsticked by Stavros. He pulled away and said, "I'd throw Maricón Reese in the ocean with rocks tied to his balls and then this would never happen."

"Yes!" cried Tracy.

Oradell said, "Tracy, why don't you go get ready to get sick."

They could feel the engines slowing, the slosh and rock of churning water. They were close to docking now.

Nikko ran in: The ambulance was waiting for them! Not much time! And he had just headed off a crisis! Doc Clyde had been coming down this way, and he had to tell him prematurely that there was something going on with Tracy Weston.

"Let's get this show on the road," said Oradell.

"Good-bye! Farewell!" Nikko threw his arms out and his head back joyously. "Into the breeches!"

Jaime had on one of Oradell's nightgowns and lots of scarves. It was time for her to get in the closet. "Jaime, sweetheart," she said, "you look great."

"I can't pay you back never."

"Pass it on, honey," she said. "Do something good for somebody else. Solidarity forever."

Things at once slowed down and sped up. Jaime got in bed under her covers, and Oradell got into the closet. She sank in the corner on a pile of robes that had slipped to the floor in the turmoil and Stavros covered her with shirts, hid her behind tunics. It was dark. She felt dizzy again, but then she had been in bed a lot. She thought,

Mike never knew that morning he was going to die. Even if someone is holding a gun to your head and clicking off the safety, part of you thinks something is going to save you. Nobody knows exactly, not in advance. Nobody knows the day or what channel.

She heard feet, the door to her cabin closed.

You worry and worry about something, and plan, and when it begins to happen in real time, it's over so fast. Taking the money from the Bosses, having the baby, leaving Harry.

It was too quiet. Was it working? Had she fallen asleep and missed the whole thing? Did Tracy scream convincingly? She heard thumping and heavy feet, panicked, thought it was Doc Clyde or Reese, but muffled voices were speaking Spanish. They bumped her closet door coming in, and for a second a sliver of light came in, then the door slipped back into place. They bumped it again going out.

That was the stretcher, she thought. He's going now. He's gone. Hot damn we're doing it. We're sneaking Jaime off the ship. They all thought it was Oradell going off: Clyde, the Captain, the Westons, the Blumes: down the gangplank, into the ambulance. The longer no one came, the more chance it was working. If no one guessed she was here, then Jaime had escaped.

She shifted her position slightly, and pressed into something soft, maybe a silk shirt. She faded, came back, cold and heavy. It was too tight in here. She thought of close dark places, of coal mines. They said Mike died in a coal mine. Her Italian grandfather died that way. Her mother died too young. Her father died of exposure to booze. She concentrated on the silky shirts and pants against her face. She shifted again and felt her cheek against something metallic, one of her metallic overblouses. So much money for a top! What if you spill ketchup on it? she had asked the sales clerk, who smiled politely. I mean it, said Oradell. What do you do? Throw out the damn thing? You wipe it off with a damp cloth, said the clerk. What about rust? asked Oradell. Oh Hell, I'll take two, in case of rust.

I can take as many as I want. I can do whatever I damn well please. And if this happens to be the end—the real end—what I pleased to do was help that little jerk Jaime.

What she'd really like was to get out of this tight closet into a warm bath, fingers and toes floating, water lapping her neck, the sea bird riding low on the air currents. You always hoped for more in your life, to live longer, to do something big. Mike had probably been sorry he hadn't done more.

Mike was taking a swim, smiling at her. She was in water too, up to her neck, smooth for the ocean, and that great black seabird riding the currents of air. It was the jaeger, floating in full and complete silence, as if the engines had been cut off, all mechanical devices stopped, the thumb of God on the pistons. Oradell sighed, and the sigh became enormous, radiated out.

"I've been in the water a long time, " she told Mike, her legs trailing down like the tentacles of a jelly fish.

Mike started to speak, but the engine sounds started up again, and he faded away. There were footsteps in the corridor. The water resumed its rolling. It was not yet her hour. Pistons rose and fell, waves lapped. The jaeger flew.

The End